Night Visit

Priscilla Masters was born in Halifax and brought up in South Wales. She now lives in Shropshire with her GP husband and two sons. She works part-time as a practice nurse and writes crime novels.

Priscilla Masters

Night Visit

This edition published in Great Britain in 2000 by
Allison & Busby Limited
114 New Cavendish Street
London W1M 7FD
http://www.allisonandbusby.ltd.uk

First published by Macmillan, 1998
in the United States of America

A catalogue record for this book is available
from the British Library

ISBN 0 7490 0349 9

Printed and bound by Biddles Limited,
Guildford, Surrey.

Acknowledgments

Every writer needs inspiration. Thank you, Phil, for being mine. Thanks too to Jane for 'her little idea' and Darley for his guidance all the way through from Alpha to Omega.

Prologue

July 1988

The child's eyelids snapped open in response to the slivers of sun across her face. Garan had not pulled the curtains quite together.

She sat up to the rhythm of the cows munching. That and the bright sun were enough to tempt her to join them so she threw the covers off and slid to the floor, hesitating only a moment before slipping her clothes over her head and fastening her sandals, then creeping downstairs. She didn't want Garan to hear because Garan would stop her.

The bolt was stiff and large for her fingers and it was even harder to shoot it open without waking them. She held her breath as the final bang echoed around the empty kitchen.

She didn't want Garan to hear. Garan would stop her. But soft snores wafting down from the bedroom reassured her.

Garan was asleep.

So she could run.

The cows stopped their munching just long enough to lift their heads and watch her pass before they bent again to resume their chewing. Dew-damp grass was slippery under her shoes as she walked through the long shadows of the cows swaying as they moved to juicier blades and she too moved away from the house as though drawn towards the dark rim of trees.

For the first time she reached the end without being pulled back. And curious, she peered through the slats in the fence. There were trees and patches of light grass, a rabbit and a bird, singing, on a branch. It was the rabbit that tempted her even though Garan had warned her.

The child glanced back at the shrouded windows.

But Garan was asleep.

Larkdale Herald December 24th 1998

LOCAL DOCTOR FIGHTS FOR LIFE
FOLLOWING VICIOUS ASSAULT

A family doctor was tonight in a critical condition after apparently being summoned to an isolated country area.

The doctor was discovered early this morning with severe head injuries after an assault described as vicious, premeditated and apparently motiveless. A claw hammer found near the scene of the crime has been sent for forensic analysis.

Detective Inspector Angela Skilton, investigating the case, commented tonight, 'It's a good job the night was fairly warm for the time of year or the doctor would have died of shock and exposure. We urge members of the public to let us know of anything suspicious they might have seen in the area of Gordon's Lane last night or for anyone who called the doctor out in the last twenty-four hours to contact us so we can exclude them from our enquiries.'

The British Medical Association said they were concerned about the increase in violent attacks on their members and were preparing guidelines to help the medical profession deal with such incidents. A spokesman said, 'Unfortunately the nature of the job puts doctors at risk from a certain sector of society who may resort to violence to get what they want. These may be addicts desperate for drugs, patients with aggressive tendencies or those suffering from psychotic illnesses. These doctor/patient confrontations may well take place with the doctor alone, in the patient's home and at night and threaten the entire concept of out of hours home visiting, particularly when the doctor is a female. We urge our members not to carry addictive drugs to minimise the risk of becoming a target for such patients.'

The name of the General Practitioner who is understood to come from a Larkdale practice has been withheld until relatives have been informed.

Police are keeping a round the clock vigil at the hospital, in the hope that the doctor will eventually regain consciousness but it is understood that a patient of the doctor's is helping the police with their enquiries.

Chapter One

I confess, I am a superstitious person. I dislike coincidence
and cracks in the pavement, black cats and walking under
ladders. I frequently touch wood. But my deepest-held
superstition concerns New Year's Eve. Perhaps it stems from
the first time I was allowed to stay up and witness the arrival
of the New Year. It sent an uncomfortable shiver up my
spine, not the glancing back at the old year but a horrid
apprehension for what the new year might bring. I think I
was about ten years old, both excited and apprehensive,
pleased at the late hour yet dreading the actual cusp of the
year. I remember that on the first stroke of twelve I asked
myself with a shiver, Am I happy? Am I really and truly
happy?

I knew that the question had huge significance because
the entire following year would be coloured by my reply.

So for the first hour of the New Year I was always filled
with apprehension, using each incident as an omen, a
jogged arm, a spilt drink, a torn dress, anger from my
father, apologies from my mother, mad, bad looks between
them. After I had qualified as a doctor I hated being on call
on New Year's Eve. But I had never worked out why. For
whom would it prove unfortunate? For me or my patients?
Would I blight them or they me?

On that particular New Year's Eve I was unlucky enough
to be on call. Looking back now I wonder if it would have
been better if I had readopted my old, childhood habit and
hidden under the bed . . .

It began at exactly twenty-two minutes past twelve on the
first of January, about an hour after we'd finally arrived at

the New Year's Eve party. We'd got there late – not because I was on duty and had been called out to a child with probable appendicitis; that hadn't been the delaying factor. A swift, textbook diagnosis, a chat with the house surgeon on call, the child's transfer to hospital accompanied by worried parents. That had been the easy, expedient part. The problem had been Robin. He hadn't been ready.

I had arrived back from the visit to find him still standing under the shower, shampooing his hair, soaping his armpits, simply standing, his head tilted upwards to meet the water cascading down his face, exactly as he had almost certainly been doing all the time I had been examining the sick child and arranging her admission to hospital. I slammed the door shut on his 'prinking and preening' as my father would have called it. But my father had been talking about girls. What the appropriate phrase would have been for a man who blow-dried his hair with the narcissism of a professional crimper, slapped on after-shave with all the generosity of a perfume sales-woman and then spent thirty minutes deciding which tie to wear I was not sure. But whatever it was my husband did it. And he was doing it now.

He looked up, aware that I was watching him. Robin always knew when someone was watching him and they frequently did – especially women.

He shot me a sly glance. 'Going like that, Harry?'

'Absolutely.' I uncoiled from the bed. 'I normally wear baggy brown skirts, loafers and thick sweaters to New Year's Eve parties.'

'Mmm.' He wasn't really listening but was still distracted by the ties and his reflection, holding up first a multi-coloured maroon and grey then a psychedelic green and lastly a sedate navy against his shirt, holding the last up a fraction longer than the others because it complimented his eyes. I knew him so well I didn't even need to watch him to realise that each time he held a tie against him he would unconsciously be smiling into the mirror.

'Prinking and preening,' I muttered. He was far too absorbed in himself to hear.

At last we were ready to descend from the bedroom. We settled the babysitter in front of the TV with cans of coke and packets of crisps, sensing her anxiety to be rid of us. Ever since she'd acquired a boyfriend she could not wait for us to go. The boyfriend was young. His clothes looked scruffy and too big for him. He stared at the carpet, flushed and refused to meet our eyes.

But Sylvie was polite. 'Have a good time. Don't do anything I wouldn't do,' she said cheekily. The boyfriend's face turned an even deeper shade of red.

Such transparent embarrassment. He'd grow out of it.

Outside Robin threw me the car keys. 'You may as well drive, Harriet. You won't be drinking much anyway – being on call.'

I had thought such bad luck might have warranted some sympathy but Robin was irritated and, I suspected, feeling sorry for himself. Bloody wife on call. New Year's Eve.

Stuff him, I thought, as I slipped the car into gear and reversed down our drive onto Larch Road.

There was a sharp frost that night which had left a dangerous satin sheen on the road. Above, a navy sky speckled with stars gave me the usual feeling of awe, beauty and insignificance and as I drove down the road I picked up the vague sounds of New Year's Eve parties all around the 'select development' where we lived. Through lit windows I could spy on stage-set parties, people laughing, people drinking around Christmas trees and people wearing silly hats. We drove past and left them all behind.

It was a quarter to twelve when we arrived at Ruth and Arthur's. And so my earlier fears had not been realised. There were still fifteen minutes to go of this old year before the new one began. On the threshold I hesitated before following Robin through.

Inside the party was in full swing with plenty of loud, cheery voices, beer spilling on the carpet, people talking with their mouths full, spitting olive stones into ashtrays. I moved through the clusters of people, aware that enough wine had been drunk for the women to start flirting in the slightly debauched way thirty-something women do, with flushed faces, bad language and midriff bulges tightly reined in. And I could anticipate the confessions which would buzz along the telephone wires the next day.

But this was a nosy little town. Plenty would not be forgiven – or forgotten.

I had barely had a drink planted in my hand before someone shouted, 'Two minutes to go.' The television was switched on, the Party Swingers CD off. There was the inevitable sound of bagpipes. Big Ben chimed. We sang 'Auld Lang Syne'. The kissing began and I was over-whelmed with a huge dissatisfaction that I knew would last all year.

We had still been pecking cheeks and wishing each other the compliments of the season when the door was flung open and a dark haired man entered. He was squat with coarse, ugly features reminiscent of the missing link and his dogstooth check suit was flashy and tasteless but expensive. He was no oil painting but while he would have been thrown out of a beauty contest his escort, following closely behind, would not. She was a slim beauty with pale, shoulder length hair good enough for a shampoo advert and a silver dress that displayed, to perfection, large, unsupported breasts, a handspan waist and slim, curving hips. The entire gathering seemed to draw breath and notice her while her blue eyes flashed around the room, sizing everyone up, males and females, until they caressed my husband and stuck there. Robin was already loosening his tie – the psychedelic green. I could have warmed my hands by the sexual tension in their gaze. I watched until it started smoking and out of mortification I switched my

13

attention back to her escort. I felt a surge of sympathy for him because I knew he was enduring the same as me. Beautiful partners are a destructive force. Hurricanes uproot trees and flatten unstable buildings. Beautiful partners wreak their own havoc. They uproot relationships and flatten egos. So I flashed him a warm, friendly smile.

Ruth sashayed towards me and flung her arms around my neck. 'Harriet, darling. A Happy New Year.'

She was pissed. Her dress had ridden far up her plump thighs and she didn't even care. Sober she would have anchored the hem firmly down. She gave a wobbly smile then dug me in the ribs.

'Potent stuff; she said with a strange, faltering wink, 'that HRT.' Her arm dropped around my shoulders.

'Delighted it agrees with you.' I was always stiff mixing work with my social life. I was never quite sure how to act – normally or responsibly – and invariably came over as distant or snobbish. I was aware that it isolated me but no one at medical school taught you how to mix with patients who regarded you as superhuman and infallible, and friends who discussed wombs and cervices at inappropriate times. I had been subjected on more than one occasion to talk of periods at dinner parties, birth control at the theatre, gastric reflux at restaurants.

'It does agree with me, Harry. It does,' she replied in her booming voice. It probably stood her in good stead at the comprehensive school where she was a headmistress but right now it was making my eardrum vibrate uncomfortably.

Quite suddenly she stopped talking and her eyes flickered around the room, deliberately not pausing on anyone – not even on the silver dress. But when they landed back on me she was frowning.

It didn't take much insight to read her mind. 'I hope you *are* having a good time,' she said, suddenly and soberly perceptive.

14

I assured her I was. I really was but it didn't fool her.

'I worry about you, Harry,' she said.

Me too.

I was silent. I could see right past her. The blonde was moving in for the kill. For minutes now she had been fluttering around the room with the good taste not to approach my husband directly, but working on widening the distance between her and Ape Man.

Robin was lounging against the wall in that half-cocked, lazy way he had, talking to my partner, Duncan. His eyes, however were directed elsewhere. In fact they had been following her around the room – like all the other men. Whoever they had been talking to they had all been eyeing the silver dress at the precise point where it ended, a good way up the slim thighs.

I moved my head to take in Duncan, my sedate, country tweed partner who had stopped watching his wife with such absorption and was contorting his neck so he too could get his eyeful. Perhaps this should have alerted me. Duncan was a straight, family man, no flirter or seducer. Yet he too was mesmerised by the girl. She even had the right laugh. When writers next describe someone's laugh as 'bell-like', believe them.

Tinkle tinkle.

But now she had reached her goal and was within touching distance of Robin. The laugh pealed a few more carillons before his eyes searched for and found me. I knew the drill inside out, upside down, backwards and forwards, word perfect.

She'd asked him whether his wife was here.

Quick work.

I sensed a rapid, professional appraisal before she turned back to him.

Even from the wrong side of the room I could read her mind.

No competition whatsoever.

Plain, stick-thin and short with straight, mousy hair and a rotten egg complexion. Plus I knew I had no flair at dressing. You see that was another thing they had neglected to teach me at medical school, the right clothes for a female medic to wear. I had such a horror of looking tarty that I stuck to safe, neutral colours, below knee skirts that ballooned over my hips. Even my party dress tonight was hardly alluring, black wool with a full skirt, a high neck, a modest length. I looked down at the thick, homely material and the low heeled shoes adorned with my one concession to the festive season – diamanté buckles. In fact, I reflected, my clothes bore so little resemblance to my actual form that I could have gained two stone and no one would have noticed – not even Robin.

Tinkle tinkle.

Especially not Robin.

I dreaded the next twelve months.

I was so sick of going to parties only to be discounted by the glamour-girls. I was sick of Robin's emotional instability, sick of the way he bounced from woman to woman, always returning to me, like a ball from the wall. I was sick of being the discarded wife. It hit me like a shovel in the chest to realise just how sick I was because there was another angle to this nausea. I was actually sick of loving him. I was physically winded by so much revelation and gave a short, noisy gasp. Luckily for me no one was near enough to notice.

It was then, right on cue, that a dark-haired woman I knew vaguely appeared from the kitchen with a fatuous grin on her face. 'Harriet,' she said, giggling, 'your handbag's making a funny noise.'

I escaped to the kitchen, glad of the diversion. The evening was deteriorating rapidly. Even a call-out had to be preferable to this humiliation and all it portended. So I welcomed the sound of the handbag bleeping insistently and fished out the small paging device I carry when I'm on

call. In response to pressure on the green button it obediently flashed up its message.

Mr Carnforth, piles bleeding, in a lot of pain.

But Mr Carnforth does not have piles. He has an inop-
erable carcinoma of the rectum which I daily expect to
perforate. And besides – I may as well stare at his rear end
as at the arsehole I'm married to.

The blonde gave me a beatific smile when I told Robin
I had to leave. Her I ignored. She reminded me a little too
much of the cat that got the cream. And Robin knew better
than to try and introduce us. Behind Robin's visage as he
met my gaze there was not a trace of responsibility. His
smile was bland and friendly and his big hands cradled the
beer glass as I knew he would be cradling the anatomy of
the blonde later on. My eyes flickered over the big breasts.
Oh maybe not tonight but at some time in the future, in
this year that had just begun so badly.

I smiled goodbye to him. Somewhere, deep down,
because I felt I understood him, I even forgave Robin. Infi-
delity was so much part of his make up. It was not a deliberate act. He simply lacked something, an understanding of
how his actions affected those around him. I suppose it was
as I left the party and walked back down the drive that I
really formulated my New Year's resolution. Robin and I
had spent our last New Year together. By this time next year
we would be divorced.

My car was reluctant to start. Buy a big, boring box of a
car that screams reliability at you from the showroom and
three years later it'll let you down on just such a cold,
January night. It coughed and failed and coughed again
but eventually like a good, doctor's vehicle it burst into life
and I turned around to head south towards the hills, the
forest and the Carnforths' smallholding.

It sat on the edge of a forest, mixed deciduous with

17

swathes of forestry pines, a rugged, beautiful place with an eerie cold stillness, especially tonight, in the first hour of a new year, one which already promised so little. As I drove slowly along the narrow lane which led to the farm I took the time to stare upwards, at the holes punched through the black sky allowing the stars to illuminate far hills iced with snow. The car slipped once or twice on frozen patches but the gritters had done their work. It wasn't until I turned up the Carnforths' lane that the car really began to have problems. I slid towards the yellow lights, drove through the open gate and pulled up on the concrete flagstones. I flicked the headlights off and reached in the back for my Gladstone bag. It was only then that I realised Vera Carnforth was standing in the doorway, holding a storm lantern and peering across the field, towards the edge of the meadow, as though she was straining to see something out there.

She didn't know I was here. For some reason I found the sight disturbing, her standing so still on this freezing night, staring. Curious, I followed her gaze but the night was black and silent. I could not even make out the outline of the trees.

There was nothing there.

I climbed out of the car, approached her as softly as though she was sleep-walking and touched her shoulder. 'Vera?'

'Aagh.' She started and swung the lantern towards me, her face white as the snow, lips bloodless.

'Did you hear something? An owl?'

How we struggle for rational explanations.

'No,' she said. 'No. I heard nothing.' Her voice cracked with disappointment. I peered through the night. 'Then what are you doing out . . .?'

She interrupted me, normality returned. 'I'm glad you've come, Doctor.' She started towards the door. 'I'm so sorry to call you out. New Year's Eve too. But he's in agony.'

18

Her face was angled with worry. 'Don't tell him,' she begged. 'Please, don't tell him.'

'Vera, I . . .'

'I don't want him knowing.' Her eyes were frightened. 'He's terrible bad.' The anticipated had happened. I should have either driven here faster or called an ambulance direct from the party. I should have used my brain but the blonde had addled it. These weren't unthinking folk, but stalwarts. They would not have called tonight except in an emergency. And this obviously was. It sounded as though 'his evil friend' as his wife called it had finally eroded a blood vessel. More work for the ambulance crew. Still, I was working on New Year's Eve. Why not them too? I would not let this brave old man bleed to death in his own home without trying everything in the medical textbook starting with a blood transfusion and a night shift of trained staff to replace his exhausted wife.

I followed her into the tiny, square sitting room which now doubled up as a bedroom and could smell the gore from the moment I entered. Carnforth was lying flat on the bed, pale-faced and shocked and in this squalid room in the second hour of the new year I sensed all our despairs, hers that he would finally 'know' and give up hope, his that he was dying, mine that I had finally failed. An old essay set during my first year at medical school rose up to leer at me. 'The function of a doctor is to tell his patients when they can expect to die and what of.' Discuss.

Young, idealistic and naive, my hackles had risen at such a cynical approach to the subject but now, after eight years of general practice, I could have dealt with the subject too well.

I met Carnforth's exhausted eyes and felt a sudden flood of exasperation. For goodness' sake. He must know the diagnosis. What could he conceivably think was wrong with him? Not piles. I peered closely at his face, pale now as a wax death mask.

He managed a feeble smile. 'Hello there, Doc. Sorry to drag you away from your party.'

I continued the banter 'No loss. It was awful anyway.' I wrapped the sphygmo cuff around his arm. 'I was glad of the opportunity to leave.' I smiled. 'Not much of a party animal.'

His blood pressure was well below legal limits, his radial pulse fluttering away like a butterfly. I lifted the quilt to peer beneath and quickly dropped it again.

Carnforth closed his eyes in pained embarrassment. 'Bit of a mess, Doc.'

I nodded. I was finding it difficult to speak. I had watched Reuben for the last six months, from the moment of diagnosis, through invasive tests, gradually getting thinner and weaker, knowing all the time that it led inexorably to this. I had even anticipated the time scale, muttering to myself that he would be lucky to see the New Year in. But he had, just. I touched his hand. 'Some people will do anything to get a nice warm hospital bed.' Carnforth gave me a steady stare. He knew what his wife didn't want him to know. Misguidedly she wanted to spare him the anguish. The whole thing was as much a game of charades as the pantomime I had left at Ruth's house and I suddenly realised how very far away that all seemed, how very false. This was reality. And the year promised plenty of both.

I stared back at Carnforth to wait for his answer. 'You're the boss,' he said and I left to use the phone in the kitchen. I had an ambulance to arrange and a junior hospital doctor to drag away from his mess party as I had been dragged from mine.

When I returned to the room Vera Carnforth was sitting on her husband's bed and I had the feeling they had been talking seriously about something. I was deceived into thinking she had at last shared her burden of knowledge with him. Tears were streaming down the old man's face and he was clutching his wife's hand. I felt an intruder.

Vera turned and I realised they had not even mentioned his illness. They had been talking about something else, something they didn't want to share with me.

'He doesn't want to leave here.' Vera gave a pathetic attempt at a smile. 'Silly, isn't he?' She kissed his sweating forehead. 'Silly old baby.'

Reuben was angry. 'You know why I don't like leaving here,' he said.

Vera gave a great sigh, moved her face close to his. 'Will you wait all your life, Reuben?'

Carnforth lifted his head with great effort but dignity too. 'If that's what it takes. Yes.' And he added, 'however long that may be.'

'Hush, Reuben,' his wife said softly and exhausted he dropped back onto the pillow.

The three of us watched for the ambulance together, easy to pick out as it climbed the valley, its great, blue arc light sweeping through the night. Even Reuben smiled as he watched it flicker across the ceiling like pixie lights. He took a last look around the farm as we wheeled him through the kitchen. He knew he wouldn't be back. As the trolley reached the kitchen door he grabbed my hand. 'Help me, Doc, please. Help me.' I had the odd feeling he did not mean his disease.

I threw Robin out one month later after finding every single cliché in the book, from long blonde hairs on his suits to lipstick on his collar.

And so my year began.

Chapter Two

It had not occurred to me that I would feel vulnerable without Robin. If I had thought at all about life without him, considering him my weakness, surely his absence would bring nothing but benefit.

I was wrong.

I felt anxious about minor problems, missed having someone to reassure me I had done the right thing at work and lay awake at night wondering where I had gone wrong in my marriage. And besides increased personal vulnerability I had changed in another way. I felt hugely, almost ridiculously responsible towards my daughter, Rosie. Not doubly protective – that would have been logical. It was far more unbalanced than that, more like twenty times more protective, and this responsibility combined with a guilty desperation to shield her from hurt.

Two weeks after he had gone she went on her first access visit, prettily dressed, I thought, in a scarlet anorak and jeans, scarlet gloves and a skiing hat. I had expected her home sometime during the evening. But halfway through the afternoon I heard a car draw up, its door slam, and the front door open, followed by running steps. It didn't take much deduction to know something had gone badly wrong. The car drew away with a sudden burst of loud pop music and the house was silent. I put my book down to listen. Soft sobs, stifled by a pillow.

I climbed the stairs and agonised outside her door for many minutes before plucking up the courage to knock.

'Rosie, Rosie …' Nothing but a wounded sniff.

I tried again, louder this time. 'Rosie.'

Another loud sniff. She peered through a half-inch crack in the door, her face mournful and tear stained.

'Can I help?'

Her face was pale and I felt a guilty, selfish beast. She brushed her eyes with her sleeve. 'He says next time can I wear a dress. He doesn't like jeans.'

My hatred of Robin made me dig my nails into the palm of my hand.

We sat glumly together on the bed, side by side, two dejected, rejected women.

'I don't like her, Mum,' she said. 'It was her who said we couldn't go to a restaurant because I was wearing jeans.' Then with sudden, forceful insight she burst out, 'I don't believe we ever were going to go to a restaurant. I think she tells lies. Daddy's never minded me wearing jeans before, has he?'

Rosie could be, at times, a very perceptive child.

So we sat like conspirators, shutting out the common enemy. We dialled a takeaway pizza that night and pigged out in front of the television, watched a childish Disney video while slurping coke straight from the can.

We revert to juvenile comforts when we are distressed.

A comfort to me was that although home was altered irrevocably, bruised and damaged beyond mere healing, work was unchanged. My two partners were kind, in their differing ways, when I finally confessed that Robin had gone. On the surface it seemed to make no difference.

Duncan was bluff, embarrassed and for some reason apologetic as though he had been party to Robin's defection merely by having been around on New Year's Eve to witness the conquest of the blonde.

But when he touched my hand and said, 'He'll be back, Harriet' in a meant-to-be reassuring, professional tone, I knew it would be better if I came clean.

'I sincerely hope not, Duncan,' I said, more sharply than I'd meant to.

But if Duncan was embarrassed by my new-found single state, Neil was far more pragmatic. But then Neil and Duncan were as far apart as the two poles. He was a dapper man, slim, slight, dark haired, always impeccably dressed in a sombre suit, polished shoes, plain ties. As a man he could have been considered cold, lacking emotion. I had rarely seen him rattled, except when his wife, and later his son, had left him. He gave me a faintly quizzical look when I blurted out my news and something of his cynical nature reached me.

'You're quite right, Harriet,' he said. 'There isn't any point struggling on. If one partner decides it's time to split the other has no option but to swim along with the tide.'

I tried the vague smile but underneath I had temporarily abandoned my own problems to wonder again. Why had Petra gone without a word to anyone?

Robin and I had dined with them at a restaurant two nights before she left. They had seemed perfectly comfortable together. There had been no hint of disharmony between them. Yet less than forty-eight hours later she had, apparently, packed her bags and walked out and ever since that day Neil had habitually worn this cynical, world-weary expression. I had heard nothing from Petra since and had, at first, been hurt. I had thought we were close friends yet she had not confided in me. It had seemed to rub in the fact that sometimes I lacked empathy. I had not known she was unhappy, and as a doctor I felt I should have. We were supposed to be able to see things that lie beneath the surface, to understand people's motives for their behaviour. I had picked up nothing and ever since then had felt in this instance at least I had missed something significant. The feeling had faded since then. Now, facing Neil, it returned, as strongly as ever.

Since she had gone I had asked Neil twice for her address or telephone number but he had, it seemed to me, been deliberately vague and I had not pursued the matter. As a salve to my conscience I had said to myself, he was my partner, therefore it was to him that I owed my loyalty. The lecture had not stopped me wondering. I seemed to remember her telling me that she had family in Birmingham. So I guessed she was there – somewhere. But Birmingham is a big city and she had never mentioned any specific district.

The whole thing had puzzled me for the last three years, especially when Sandy, their only son, had followed his mother. He had been fourteen years old when he had left, almost a year to the day after his mother. Neil had muttered something about him missing Petra and wanting to join her. That had been his sole explanation. But he never even visited although father and son had been skin close. And I had watched as Neil's face grew more lined and preoccupied. He never even talked about them now.

'Things do get better, Harriet.' It seemed that his brown eyes were telling me much more than just a simple sentence. They still contained emptiness, loneliness and puzzlement too. I was tempted to pat his shoulder back. Instead I smiled my thanks, picked up my consultation notes and escaped to my morning's surgery.

I invariably felt a vague pleasure on entering my consulting room. It was so different from Duncan's homely, shabby room strewn with photographs, books and medical journals or Neil's clinical atmosphere, empty: white surfaces, surgical instruments. Their desks were different too, Duncan's a shabby, oak roll top, 1920s, Neil's a wide expanse of grey formica, equipment contained in cupboards. Mine was a modern piece of pine, books and equipment neatly ordered. My room reflected my own tastes. It was small and square with a window which overlooked the back garden – when it was open. Closed it was covered with regulation frosted glass. Naked people do not like an audience.

There was the obligatory computer, two chairs and an examination couch as well as a red plastic table and some toys planted to entertain children while I spoke to their mothers. The carpet was beige, the curtains a riot of yellows, greens and orange, tropical flowers meant to distract the patient while I interviewed or examined them. There were pictures of Rosie, one of myself on an early walking holiday with Robin. The overall effect was of warmth and empathy but order too. In fact, the atmosphere of clinical order was something I yearned for; even, occasionally, at home.

Before pressing the buzzer to summon my first patient I logged on to the computer, leaned back in my chair and closed my eyes, suddenly apprehensive about my long-term future. The New Year had beckoned darkly. There were still months to go before the fates would change. And then what? Was there just to be me and Rosie? And when she grew up would there then be just me, alone? A wave of sadness hovered over my head. I was wishing now that I had not lost my baby, my son, Robin's child.

Physician, I whispered, heal thyself. Never mind the others. I eyed the toppling pile of notes in my basket. How could I hope to heal them when sick at heart myself?

And for me there was no one to listen.

I pressed the buzzer for my first patient. It was Vera Carnforth, looking years older since the funeral, leathered pouches underneath both her eyes. She looked tired, worn out. Reuben had lasted less than forty-eight hours in hospital. Blood transfusions, medical care, the attentions of nurses. He had descended into unconsciousness. Nothing had saved him as we had both known as we had watched him being loaded into the bright yawn of the ambulance.

But had he known?

It was that memory that haunted me now. I had failed in my duty to Reuben Carnforth. I should have respected him as a man, discussed his shortening future, planned for the final hours. It was part of my duty as a doctor; part of the programme of continuing care, cradle to grave. I watched her fingers knot through the handles of an old fashioned, brown plastic shopping bag and realised that however well she blended against the backdrop of Cattle's Byre she looked out of place here. Shabby and worn, tired, muddy. And there clung to her the faint scent of the cowshed even though she was wearing her town clothes.

As I studied her my initial instinct was to print out a prescription for Prozac. It would have put a thick sheet of opaque glass between her and her unhappiness but she forestalled me.

'I don't want none of your happy pills, Doctor. There's no answers there.'

I felt scolded and guilty, empty handed and powerless with nothing better to trot out than the tired old cliché, that he'd had a good life.

It provoked a fierce reaction. The bag was put on the floor to leave both hands free to clench into fists. 'You think that? That my Reuben had had a good life?'

'But surely – the farm, the animals.' I was floundering. 'You always seemed so contented together. I thought . . .' I was at a loss for words. The truth was I had not thought – anything.

'Help me, Doctor.'

Vera was finding it difficult to continue. 'We had a cursed life, Doctor,' she said at last. 'True. We could have been happy. We had a lot once, a farm stocked with healthy animals, each other.'

'Children?'

A frozen expression set her face hard as a night frost. 'One son,' she said, 'but we don't see him any more.'

I was surprised. Vera had always struck me as a calm, peaceable woman, not the sort to quarrel with her only son. Yet on reflection I realised she was telling the truth. She did not see her son. I had never seen anyone visit Reuben either at home or in hospital. There had only ever been her, sitting at his bedside, holding his hand. So the family rift had been both deep and permanent.

Unless. 'Abroad?'

She swallowed painfully. 'We haven't had anything to do with our son for nearly ten years,' she said. 'We posted him Christmas cards. Birthday cards too. But he doesn't send one back.'

'Surely he came to his father's funeral?'

She shook her head and tried to hide her glistening eyes by rubbing her fingers across her eyebrows.

'You quarrelled?'

'In a way. He entrusted something to us.' The sentence hung in the air but I had learned not to prompt people too hard. If they wanted to confide in you they would.

I waited but her lips were pressed tightly together. I would probably find out later. Not now. I risked a swift glance firstly at my watch and then at the thick batch of notes. 'Look,' I said finally, 'I can't bring Reuben back from the dead, Vera. Neither can I heal family rifts. I'm just a doctor. I can offer you one of three things, a prescription, referral to a counselling agency or a chat.' My computer flashed at me. Another patient had arrived in surgery. 'But I haven't got much time this morning. I'm sorry.' Another failed consultation. It was her cue to leave but she ignored it.

'Make a longer appointment one afternoon.'

I tried to blot out the fact that her mouth was still twisted with grief and tried another tack. 'I think a break from the farm would help. You have some friends you could stay with?'

Her jaw tightened with determination. 'We got into the habit years ago of never leaving the place for long.' Her eyes, hurt with the rejection, met mine. 'I still don't like to.'

'Come and see me,' I urged, 'when I have more time.'

Without either a word or a glance she left.

The rest of my surgery went smoothly enough, routine monitoring of various chronic conditions, one or two casual callers with backache and the usual children with temperatures.

When Fern Blacklay, the receptionist, brought me in my morning coffee I used the time to dictate some referral letters before, refreshed, I picked up the next set of notes and inwardly groaned as I noticed the fluorescent sticker.

We used the code to warn ourselves. Drug addicts may be a legitimate part of the GP's workload but we have all learned to treat them with caution. Many were youngsters desperate for kicks to stave off frustrated teenage energy but some were hopelessly addicted without the volition to ever kick the habit.

Like Reuben they would eventually die of their condition.

That was their problem. Not ours. What troubled us were the means they used to finance their expensive habits, stealing anything they could lay their hands on in the surgery, not just needles and syringes and drugs but handbags, once an expensive coat. Even a nebuliser had vanished the day after one addicted 'jackdaw' had called in for a sick note to avoid doing his community service. So we doctors had to double up as police while they were around and had dreamed up a set of rules, that the receptionists should watch them the entire time they were in the waiting area and that the doctor should never leave them alone in the consulting room.

Danny was slow to respond to my calling his name.

A couple of minutes ticked by and I was contemplating calling him again although I knew he might have simply walked out. Some of the addicts quickly grew fidgety and impatient hanging around for their turn. They would pace around the waiting room, abuse the receptionists and frequently storm out – to everyone's relief. There was something unpredictable about them that made other people afraid to make contact. Mothers snatched their babies out of their prams and hugged them close. The elderly would slide away along the bench seats while the receptionists eyed them warily from behind the glass screen. The unease would spread so everyone entering the waiting room took the long way round to avoid walking past them. I had witnessed it myself. It was as though they were surrounded by an aura of restlessness.

I was about to give Danny one more call when the door was shoved open and he sauntered in.

'Good morning, Danny.'

I would be asked later, 'Did you dislike the deceased?' 'And I would answer as honestly as I could. 'No. I did not dislike the deceased.'

Pale, spotty, scruffily dressed in an ancient and smelly long coat, Danny dropped into the chair.

'So what's the problem?'

'I need some more methadone.'

Methadone is the magic substance supposed to help addicts kick their habit. Only it does nothing of the sort. The truth is that most of them supplement their prescribed methadone with illegally obtained heroin or anything else they can lay their shaking hands on. There is only one way to avoid being the cheapest drugs dealer in town and that is to flatly refuse to prescribe the addicts anything. It is better to do a blanket referral to a substance abuse unit and let them sort out these human messes.

Danny knew he was breaking the rules.

'Sorry, Danny,' I said. 'You know the score. You'll get nothing from me. When are you next due at Substance Abuse?'

'Friday,' he said pleasantly. 'And I'll never last till then.'

I wasn't playing ball. 'But they give you enough for a week.'

He stopped looking at the floor.

I have learned that addicts never look straight at you

except when they are lying. They break all normal rules of communication. We have to relearn all our instincts. Addicts never look more innocent than when they are attempting to deceive you and squeeze a couple of extra fixes out of the benevolent National Health Service.

'I met a friend,' he said. 'He was going bananas.' Another pleasant smile. 'I felt sorry for him. Gave him a couple of days' of my own supply.'

Addicts are inventive too. But it's safest to play along.

'That was very nice of you, Danny, but it means you've let yourself go short.'

'Bloody typical,' he grumbled. 'You do a friend a favour and where does it get you?'

'Bloody typical,' I echoed. 'Unfair, isn't it?'

He eyed me suspiciously. 'I'll get withdrawal.'

'If I were you, Danny,' I said, 'I would take myself down to Dr McKinley and see what you can wheedle out of him. OK?'

'You're my doctor,' he snarled. 'I got a problem. I need somethin' for it.'

My eyes wandered towards the panic button. 'You're right on one point, Danny,' I said. 'I am your doctor.'

He thumped his grubby, bony fist on my desk, making the stack of notes hop.

'I want my methadone. OK?'

'No it isn't OK,' I said. 'You know the score. We've told you before. I am your doctor. And as your doctor I have a clear, contractual agreement.' I had stopped caring whether he knew what the word contractual meant.

'Did you dislike Danny Small, Doctor?'

'No . . . No . . . No.'

'My duty is towards your health, not helping you with a habit which is slowly destroying it.'

He looked at me with cold, dead eyes. Then came the threat. He stood up, leaned right over me. 'Just pray you don't meet me one dark night, Doctor.'

I struggled to regain my composure after Danny had gone, but the encounter had left me drained and depressed. I was glad that I had reached my last patient for the morning.

Doctors read a set of notes as a fortune teller reads tea leaves. And this set was wafer thin, ergo they belonged to someone who visited the doctor infrequently. One did not have to be Sherlock Holmes to deduce this. But I could read more. This man was neither neurotic nor unhealthy. And I could read still more. The name was unfamiliar and so was the address, one I had never visited. So the entire family hardly needed the services of a doctor. I did not even recognise the road. So either his neighbours too did not summon the doctor; or they belonged to one of the other lists in Larkdale or he had no neighbours. I felt pleased with my deductions and memories of Danny began to fade.

I shook the loose leaves out of the folder and read both name and date of birth. Anthony Pritchard, aged fifty-four. Last consultation ten years ago for a dog bite. There was no record of stitching or hospital admission but someone had recorded a tetanus jab.

So what had brought him here today?

I pressed the buzzer.

Patients have various ways of approaching the doctor. Some march in boldly, almost aggressively, barging in without knocking and dropping into the chair as they blurt out the reason for the consultation. Others are timid, rapping softly on the door and hesitating before they dare enter.

We have the power to frighten people. Minor conditions are magnified. Piles become cancers. Pleurisy a heart attack. Anxiety becomes any malignant condition in the medical textbook.

It didn't take me long to classify Anthony Pritchard. He was one of the timid ones, unsure and tentative. His first knock was so soft I wasn't sure I had heard anything. For good measure I did call out, 'Come in' and the door handle moved slightly. I called out again, my eye on the handle.

There was a second tap and the door opened wider. A man was hovering on the threshold, a plump man with a suet pudding face and thick, bottle-bottom glasses.

'Mr Pritchard?'

'Yes. That's right. I am he.'

A monotonic local accent, a wordy, pedantic way of speaking and an irritating, nasal voice. Not a good start.

'Come in,' I said. 'Sit down.' One gets used to directing the proceedings.

He closed the door behind him and perched on the edge of the seat.

His trousers were too tight, plump thighs straining against the stitching. Navy blue with a grey stripe. Remnants of earlier days before his legs had encased themselves in wads of fat. Either that or from a charity shop. There were plenty of those in Larkdale. His shirt also looked either vintage seventies or charity shop, yellowed Bri-nylon, frayed at the cuffs. Over that he wore a brown, tweed jacket.

I gave him an encouraging smile. 'And what can I do for you, Mr Pritchard?'

As I moved through the preliminaries I was scrutinising him. There were no obvious signs of disease. He was pale but not breathless, sweating slightly but the surgery was overheated. Maybe he was a candidate for an early coronary. I wouldn't have swapped his cholesterol level for mine. There was a lardy look about his face. And I couldn't imagine him taking much exercise. He was the sort of heavy hipped, amorphous man who had not been born to be an athlete. He had been put on this earth to pick away at details in front of a small, unobtrusive desk, sitting at the back of a dark, poky office.

I also noted that he was nervous and needed prompting so I asked him again. 'What seems to be the trouble?'

He wriggled his glasses up his nose and gave an ingratiating smile. Even that didn't do him any favours. He had bad teeth.

'I . . . wondered if you'd mind taking my blood pressure.'

Ten years, I thought, since you last consulted a medic and you've come in today to have your blood pressure checked? I was honour bound to ask him a few more searching questions.

'Have you been having problems? Headaches, tiredness, spots before the eyes?'

Again that smile. He shook his head.

'No aches or pains?'

Another shake of his head. Another smile. Another glimpse of brown, irregular teeth.

So with nothing to go on I asked him to remove his jacket and roll up his sleeve.

His top lip was beaded with sweat as he asked me which one.

'Let's try the one nearest the sphyg, shall we?' It was recognisable medical jollity, of the type they do teach at medical school.

Rolling up his sleeves made the doughy fingers tremble so much I would have offered to do it for him had it not been for a nauseating smell of body odour. And now I knew another fact about Mr Pritchard. He was not fussy about personal hygiene. It took him ages to tuck the sleeve up his arm, one slow pleat after another while I tried to stem my impatience. I was unaccountably anxious to end the consultation. Eventually the manoeuvre was complete, the sleeve displaced well above the elbow and he rested the limb across my desk so I could wrap the cuff around it and pump up the bulb. Slowly I let the cuff down, my eyes fixed on the column of mercury until it reached the bottom. Then I unhooked the stethoscope from my ears.

I might have known the level would be raised. The signs had all been here. Fat, lazy, greedy. The trouble was it was not up enough for me to commence treatment. A few lifestyle changes should be enough. But he was only fifty-four years old and age would exacerbate it. I needed to probe into his family history.

'Are your mother and father alive and well, brothers and sisters?'

'I have no brothers or sisters.' He coughed. 'I am an only child. My mother is alive,' he said carefully, 'though quite elderly and a little infirm.'

'And your father?'

'My father, unfortunately, is dead.'

'What of?'

I wasn't asking out of idle curiosity. If Pritchard's father had died young from a heart attack, combine that with his son's elevated blood pressure and it would mean we should keep an eye on things, maybe start medication earlier. My fingers were poised over the computer to feed in father's cause of death. There was a long silence. I looked up.

'Unfortunately,' he said, 'my father died from taking some poison.'

Now I was curious. 'You mean he swallowed something accidentally?'

Pritchard pursed his lips together primly. 'I couldn't really tell you that.' He gave another irritating smile. 'I was only six years old at the time. My mother doesn't like to talk about it,' he said apologetically. 'And you can't really blame her, can you? It's a skeleton in the cupboard sort of thing. So I tend not to ask her such a personal detail.' He beamed at me, pleased at his sensitivity.

But there was a potential risk factor, though not of heart disease. The offspring of suicides have a higher incidence of following suit than the general population.

'Did your father take the poison deliberately?'

'I've told you,' he said. 'I really couldn't say. He might have.' He must have picked up some of my concern

35

because he leaned forward anxiously. 'Is my blood pressure all right?'

I shrugged. 'It's a bit high. Look – I think we'd better run a few tests, cholesterol and a couple more. Book in with the nurse and I'll recheck it in a month's time. Is that all right?'

I was ready for him to put his jacket back on as another waft of BO caught me but, like Vera, he too seemed reluctant to leave. 'Are there any implications to my blood pressure being slightly high?'

I stood up. 'Let's talk about that when we have the results of your tests. In the meantime you might try and lose a bit of weight. Take some exercise, a good, brisk walk.'

I might have added, 'with a dog', but I remembered the dog bite and the tetanus jab, ten years ago. It had been a long time since he had visited a doctor. So why had he really come today? Surely not for a routine blood pressure check?

Another waft of BO as he slotted his arms back into the jacket. 'Thank you, Doctor.' He held out his hand for me to shake it.

It would have been rude not to.

Chapter Three

Duncan, Neil and myself usually met after our morning surgery, ostensibly to share out the visits but really for a cup of coffee and a chat. At least Neil and I found plenty to talk about. Duncan was more taciturn. Usually he would sit with his hands wrapped around the mug, staring moodily into his coffee, miles away. Sometimes he would interject but I had the feeling that he only threw in an argument to be controversial. An intensely private man, it could be hard to know what he was thinking.

This morning I opened the conversation with my grouse about Danny Small. 'He's getting a real nuisance. Came in demanding extra methadone. Said he'd lent some of his to a friend.'

The three of us gave the same smile, cynical, disbelieving. And that was the trouble. We never believed them, never trusted them. Even when sometimes they were telling the truth.

'They never learn, do they?' Neil's deep voice displayed intense anger. 'I usually refuse to see them at all. Bloody pests.'

Duncan spoke quietly from the corner. 'We can't refuse to see them as long as they're on our list.'

'Then get rid of the lot of them. Let some other doctor shoulder the problem.'

'Not while I'm here,' Duncan said slowly. 'We have an obligation.'

Neil's 'Pah' expressed his sentiments forcefully.

Duncan spoke again. 'Anyway, Neil,' he said, even more quietly. 'For all your fine words you do see them. I saw Danny coming out of your room a week or so ago. And I didn't notice a flea in his ear.'

Neil covered his discomfort with a smile. 'Well, he is one

of our patients, Duncan. What else can I do? As you've so rightly pointed out. We do have an obligation to see them.'

Duncan continued to watch Neil with one of his quizzical looks but this time he said nothing.

It was up to me to halt the sparring. 'I honestly thought once they all realised they'd get nothing out of us that they'd stop drifting in and making such nuisances of themselves.'

Neil frowned. 'They never stop.'

But again Duncan made a quiet challenge. 'You think not one of them reforms?'

'No.' Neil's jaw was clenched so tightly I could see his masseter muscles twitching.

'That's just not true.' Duncan finished his coffee. 'You are such a cynic, Neil. I think sometimes you forget that we're doctors. We aren't the police and we're not the politicians. We have a duty to help people.'

'If they want to be helped.'

Duncan stood up then. 'Our work is to maintain contact and hold their trust in the hope that we can eventually influence them to kick the habit.'

Neil snorted. 'And if you believe that.'

They were still glaring at one another. Again it fell to me to play peacemaker. 'I had a strange character in today,' I said. 'A guy in his fifties named Pritchard, Anthony Pritchard.'

They both looked blank.

'Name doesn't ring a bell.'

'I didn't think you'd know him. He hasn't been near the place for years.'

We all smiled, the tension melting, knowing we depended on such sparers of the over-stretched Health Service. Without them the system would collapse.

'So what brought him in today?'

The honest answer would have been, 'I don't know.' Instead I said, 'He wanted his blood pressure checked.'

I had all their attention now.

Duncan spoke first. 'And was it high?'

'Yes, a bit.' I drank some more of my coffee. 'But he couldn't have known that. Not enough to justify his first visit for ten years. It seemed a flimsy excuse.'

'So what's strange about him, Harriet?'

It was typical of Duncan that he took my comment seriously.

Neil's face creased. 'Sometimes I think there's something strange about all our patients.'

It was Duncan's comment that I answered. 'I don't know,' I said. 'He was dishevelled and sat uncomfortably close. Apart from that there wasn't really anything I could put my finger on, except one rather odd statement he made.'

They were both watching me. 'It's probably nothing,' I said, 'but when I asked him about the health of his parents do you know what he said?' I didn't even wait for them to shake their heads. 'He told me his father was poisoned. Or at least . . .' I frowned. 'What he actually said was that his father died after taking poison. He didn't specify whether it was an accident or suicide.'

'Maybe there is something in his strangeness,' Duncan commented. 'Psychologists do advise us to delve into childhood for problems in an adult.'

'I know.'

He pressed his fingers together. 'But I don't remember any cases of poisoning except a two-year-old who drank some bleach, do you, Neil?'

Neil shook his head. 'When was this?'

'Before your time. He said it was when he was six years old. That would have been about 1950. Years before either of you two came here.'

Duncan, always humanitarian, murmured, 'An unpleasant death, poor thing.'

But Neil was more interested in the medical aspect.

39

'What poison was it?'

I shrugged. 'I don't know.'

'Must have been something pretty strong to have killed him.' Neil had a love of surgical precision.

'And the coroners always err on the side of accidental death anyway. Spares the family. So it could have been a suicide.'

Neil cleared his throat with a dry cough. 'So what is so strange about this Pritchard person?'

'Do you remember the creepy Uriah Heep?' I asked.

'Dickens?'

'Yes. You know what a slime ball he was?'

Neil laughed. 'I think I'm getting the picture.'

Duncan stood up to go, 'Well you have had a morning, Harriet,' he said. 'Uriah Heep and Danny Small all in one morning.'

'I only hope my visits are less bothersome,' I said. 'It's half term and I've promised to take Rosie swimming. Besides the babysitter wants to go somewhere this afternoon. She'll be itching to leave.'

'Swimming?' Neil looked surprised. 'In February?'

'I have to do something with her,' I said and followed Duncan out of the room.

Neil caught up with me as I was walking down the stairs. 'Look, Harriet,' he said. 'I haven't liked to intrude before but is child care a problem?'

'Sometimes,' I admitted.

'I can keep an eye on Rosie for you occasionally.' He gave an awkward laugh. 'I always was fond of kids. I could manage a couple of evenings, or I could pick her up from school on my half day.'

Like a flood I realised how much he missed his son. 'Thanks, Neil,' I said. 'That'd be great. A real help. Robin . . .' I was floundering.

He grinned. 'No problem.' I caught a waft of soapy cleanliness as he passed me on the stairs.

The visit took longer than I'd anticipated, an unexpected admission to hospital for a child with an asthmatic attack. When I arrived he was pale, wheezing, exhausted, hardly able to string two words together. And there was an ugly acceptance of losing the struggle. I nebulised him, gave him some intravenous steroids and clamped the oxygen mask over his face while his mother dialled the ambulance.

I arrived home an hour after the promised one o'clock and Rosie was cross. She was standing in the doorway with her hands on her hips, her mouth puckered partly in disapproval, partly in distress. I had never had it brought home so clearly to me that the extra burden of responsibility and vulnerability was not all carried on my shoulders. Rosie suffered it too.

'Sylvie wants to go.'

Even in the few minutes it took to sort out Sylvie's money I could sense the atmosphere. The boyfriend was lounging against the door; obviously ready to leave and I noticed that she didn't ask whether I needed her the following morning. It was left to me to prompt, 'Tomorrow then,' which provoked a swift, warning glance from the boyfriend. He shrugged and she said, 'May as well,' with a distinct lack of enthusiasm.

This was only half term. There were lots of school holidays in a year. She would not come for much longer. And then what?

I watched them go down the path with a feeling of resentment. I had difficulties enough without Sylvie playing hard to get. It wasn't until I started to prepare lunch with Rosie peering over my shoulder resentfully, that I was struck by a revelation.

Maybe it wasn't just the boyfriend who was putting Sylvie off my daughter. Maybe it was something to do with the new and difficult Rosie.

I had known she would change when Robin went but she was only nine years old, an innocent and so far sheltered

41

child. Yet even with my blind, maternal love I could not deny that she was shedding her innocence and visibly changing, outwardly toughening to conceal the fact that inwardly she was doubly vulnerable.

There were other clues. Her school friends were different. Gone were all the middle class kids whose mothers had dropped them off leaving their fathers to pick them up in their Mercs and BMWs exactly three hours later; always on time.

In their place was a new breed, kids who wore designer clothes and had their ears pierced, kids who wolfed down beefburgers in spite of the BSE/CJD scare and constantly complained that they were bored.

Kids who sneered when I suggested they play Monopoly on a rainy afternoon. And there were no parents in sight – these kids walked home through the rain without coats unless I offered to drive them.

Rosie did not really blend with these new, streetwise friends. She was too naive.

So it was essential I did things with her, took her to the pictures, swimming, walking, cycling, anything to stop her from realising that although her father could claim access to her every single weekend he rarely did. In two months he had seen her twice. And then just for Saturday afternoons. Robin had dropped right out of her life leaving an unfill-able hole. Damn him. Rosie was not a toy but a real, suffering child. His daughter. But of course Robin was as oblivious to her hurt as he had always been to mine.

Chapter Four

Easter was late that year; falling at the end of a cold April. Somewhere in the middle of the month Rosie asked me if I would go shopping with her on a Saturday afternoon. She wanted a new dress. And even though I knew we were buying it for her to win Robin's approval I agreed to go with her.

After the baking central heating of the store it was cold on the pavement. Spring seemed to be particularly late that year. Maybe it would not bother at all. Maybe this winter would extend to meet the next and there would be no bright, warm season in between. Merely grey and cold followed by more grey and cold. Even the few daffodils around in tubs along the pedestrian way were spindly, hot-house things. And the crocuses had spent just that bit too long buried beneath the snow and had lost their bloom.

Rosie dawdled along the road then stopped in front of what looked like a bundle of rags. It was a beggar.

'Oh the poor thing,' she said, fumbling for my hand which I had shoved deep into my coat pocket. 'Mum, the pooor thing.'

It took me a minute or two to realise that she was not talking about the beggar; the heap of filthy rags tumbled across the pavement behind a sheet of cardboard:

PLEASE HELP I'M STARVING.

He'd got a manky kitten from somewhere and it was peeping out, wide-eyed, from the coat pocket.

And then I recognised him. Danny was staring at the pavement, seeming oblivious to the passing people who in turn seemed oblivious to him. The cap on the floor held no more than four two-pence pieces.

Rosie had dropped to her knees and was stroking the cat, murmuring sweet things. 'Oh, you poor little thing. You lovely, lovely thing. Aren't you?' The kitten gave a soft mew and climbed weakly out of Danny's coat. Danny himself was still staring at the pavement. I could not be sure he had recognised me.

Rosie was holding the kitten now and it seemed to stir Danny. He looked up, eyed Rosie stroking the pathetic creature and spoke. 'You like him, do you?'

She nuzzled her face against the fur. 'Yes,' she said. 'He's lovely.'

'Would you like him?'

'I'd love him.'

'Then you can have him,' he said, 'for a fiver.'

Rosie stood up and faced me, holding the kitten very tightly. 'Please give him the money,' she said.

'But Rosie . . .'

A couple of fixes, a hit of cocaine, a day's marijuana smokes?

So would Danny get the money out of me one way or another? Using my daughter? I felt angry.

But Rosie was pale and determined. 'I think the kitten,' she said, 'will have a better life with me.'

Resentfully I fumbled in my bag and drew out a five-pound note, handed it to Danny and knew whatever the sign said he would not buy food with it. He grasped it with a mittened hand, fingernails encrusted with filth, before giving me a hard stare. 'Nice of you, Doctor,' he sneered. 'Look after it properly, won't you?'

I nodded, ignoring the dig. But at the same time I was looking at the placard. It struck me then that the apostrophe was in the right place. The spelling was correct. Danny should have been no down and out. He was literate at the very least. There were jobs in the town. Not for drug addicts.

The future rumbled towards me.

'Did you dislike the deceased?'

'No. I did not dislike the deceased but I resented the time wasted dealing with drug addicts.'

And the pompous words.

'We are trained to deal with genuine sickness. Not self abuse.'

The kitten brought a new air of homeliness to the house once we had taken it to the vet, had it treated for fleas, given it a couple of jabs and fed it. It was a sweet, playful animal which Rosie named Tigger. Its connection with Danny Small was soon forgotten.

So the month passed a little more pleasantly, slowly warming to the promise of sunshine and summer until the week before Maundy Thursday. At the back of my mind I knew that at some time Anthony Pritchard would come back to have his blood pressure checked and his results explained. Normally I would be unaware of follow up dates, leaving the appointment-making to the patient – or client as we were encouraged to think of them. Personally I thought the word a bit of a climb down. Prostitutes had clients. Surely doctors had patients? But Anthony Pritchard felt more like a client than a patient.

It is never a good idea to create a prejudice against the patient. Our job is not to like or dislike them but to treat them. As a rule I did not find that a difficult maxim to follow. I did not intend breaking good habits. That was the vow I made as I picked his notes out of the basket, pressed the buzzer and listened for his steps.

The knock on the door startled me. I had not heard him approach. Like a ghost walking there had been no footsteps. I called out, 'Come in.'

Pritchard's face appeared around the edge of the door, smiling, a comedy character, with me still directing the proceedings. 'Come right in, Mr Pritchard. Sit down.'

The humble smile never faltered and I formed the rogue thought: a man like this could really irritate you.

45

What I had not yet learned was that a man like this could also intimidate you. Softness, hesitance and intrusion could, at times, feel as threatening as aggression.

He had a strange, disconnected walk, heavy and untidy, knocking against the side of my desk as he sat down, blinking like an owl in the daylight. Even then it crossed my mind that I would almost have preferred it if he had done a Danny Small on me, shouted or sworn, demanded, threatened. At least I always knew what Danny wanted. Instead Pritchard peered at me through his thick glasses.

What did he want?

I put the blood results down in front of him to explain they were normal. He leaned forward, crossed his legs and I caught a waft of the familiar stale sweat smell.

His trousers today were not tight but they were too short, displaying flabby ankles. His jacket was grubby brown Harris tweed, the kind that never goes out of date. So they say. I have my suspicions that it never was in date. His shirt was old fashioned, seventies flowers, the tie narrow and carelessly washed, its crumpled lining visible. And yet I had the uncomfortable feeling that he had dressed up to come and see me today. That these were his smart clothes. And that he was self-consciously proud of them, beaming at me, inviting comment and he was fingering the lapel of the jacket, deliberately drawing attention to it.

The actions embarrassed me so I took my eyes off him to fix on the computer screen. 'Your blood results are all right,' I repeated, 'although your cholesterol is a touch higher than we'd like.'

He was still beaming at me, his eyes magnified through the thick lenses. Did he understand what I was saying?

I tried again. 'You could do with adopting a low-fat diet. Why don't I make you an appointment to see our dietician?'

I knew exactly what I was doing. I was deliberately trying to divert Pritchard's care away from me. Call it superstition

46

or call it instinct but I wanted to avoid him. No, that is too weak a phrase. Rather I knew I *must* avoid him.

The trouble was that behind his glasses his eyes were penetrating both my actions and my motives. He knew exactly what I was up to. 'I don't think I really need to see the dietician,' he said, 'Harriet.'

I stiffened.

It may seem insignificant that a patient calls you by your Christian name. But the title 'doctor' is an amulet. It spins a magic web around you. You can ask a man intimate questions about his sex life, chat easily to him about extra marital affairs – all with impunity, while you have the title 'doctor' wrapped around you. Without it I was embarrassingly vulnerable.

And how did he know my name was Harriet? My title throughout the surgery was Doctor H. Lamont. Only friends call me Harry or Harriet. Pritchard was not my friend. It felt an intrusion.

He was already taking his jacket off, hanging it over the back of the chair, pleating his shirt sleeve. 'You'll be wanting to check my blood pressure again,' he said, 'I expect.' The fat, white arm lay across my desk. I had no option.

So for the second time I put the diaphragm of the stethoscope over the brachial pulse and pumped the cuff up. His blood pressure was still up. In fact it was slightly higher.

'You need medication,' I said shortly, typing the script into the computer, struggling to ignore the smell of armpits. Did he ever wash?

His arm was still lying across my desk like a grub. I instructed him how and when to take the tablets and told him to make an appointment to see the practice nurse. I even made a joke of it. 'An excellent young woman by the name of Miriam.' And for good measure I added, 'You'll like her.'

47

He gave another of those quietly focused smiles. 'I'd much rather come back and see you.'

'That isn't necessary, Mr Pritchard.' It was almost as brutal as physically pushing him away. 'The nurse can easily deal with it. It's just a minor problem.'

He stood up then. 'Then I'll make another appointment,' he said.

I noticed he didn't say who with.

He had almost reached the door when he paused with his hand on the handle. 'Oh by the way,' he said. 'You were asking about my poor father.'

'Only his cause of death,' I said sharply.

'I felt I should question my mother as to the exact circumstances of my father's death,' he said. 'Unfortunately it appeared to upset her.'

'I'm sorry,' I said. 'I didn't mean you to.'

'But you wanted to know.'

'I was only interested from a medical aspect.'

'I asked her anyway,' he said.

'And?'

'Apparently,' he said, 'at the time, the coroner classed it as an accident.'

I wasn't surprised and didn't feel the need to point out that coroners prefer accidents to suicides. It was kinder to the relatives. An intent to die is difficult to prove without an announcement, a letter or a history of depression.

He hovered in the doorway. 'There is another thing that my mother told me, in confidence, which I feel I should mention.'

'Yes?' Despite myself I felt a salacious curiosity.

He flicked his tongue over his lips, a lizard waiting for an insect. 'Let's just say she wasn't sorry he didn't come out of the hospital – except feet first.'

Chapter Five

It was a month later, on a perfect spring day, when clouds billowed across a deep blue sky that I made my next move to exorcise the ghosts of New Year's Eve. I had a particular reason for thinking about them today. It was Robin's birthday and in a moment of weakness I had sent him a card. I came out of surgery, felt the sun on my face and believed that not only could I acknowledge Robin's existence but also I could face Vera Carnforth again. And this time back at Cattle's Byre.

I drove through the town, turned off the main road and crossed a narrow causeway over twin pools. Locally they were known as the Heron Pools and today they looked particularly inviting, each cloud contrasting very distinctly in the dark glass of its surface. Ferns and rushes dipped into the water, breaking its surface so the cloud picture was not quite perfect but fringed and in the border colour was returning to the country with the vivid pinks and yellows of wild flowers and waving above them trees in bridal blossom. Once over the causeway I turned right, immediately climbing through the dense woodland until the lane flattened out and I reached the Carnforths' small-holding. As I pulled up in the yard I reflected for a moment. It was just five months since I had last been here, glad to be summoned from the party and rescued from the role of pitied wife. It seemed in the distant past but to myself I could admit I still thought of Robin. And Rosie did too, often. I gripped the steering wheel in sudden tension. Had it been worth it? When five months later I longed to see him, even if only to reassure myself that I had shed that awful, mooning love. What had I done by throwing him out? Had I finally pushed him that extra distance into a relationship with Janina?

Robin had severed connections a little too completely. He never even rang. Arrangements to see Rosie were invariably left on my answering machine and not even addressed to me. 'Rosie, darling. It's Daddy here. How about Saturday?' His usual instructions. 'Wear something decent. We'll go out somewhere.' Never even a mention of me. No 'Love to Mummy' or any other message.

I had a sudden, strong impulse to know how Robin was. You can't have a close relationship with someone for more than ten years and then let their place be a void. I took my key out of the ignition. Maybe coming here had rekindled my feeling for him. Maybe it was just too soon. And five months and a different season had not been enough after all.

To try and bring back my negative feeling about him I concentrated hard on Rosie. He saw too little of her. He was neglectful.

I closed my eyes, and wished things had turned out otherwise. Irritated with myself I picked my Gladstone bag off the passenger seat and opened the car door to yet another doubt.

Why had I really come here to see Vera? Had it merely been to lay a ghost? But what did I presume I had to offer her? She was not ill, as far as I knew. She didn't need a doctor.

So why did the doctor need her?

She had not consulted me. So why had I really come? To offer bereavement counselling? I wished I could have told her, with conviction, that Reuben was smiling down on her, that he was happy, that he was out of pain and in a better place but I was a doctor, not a medium, not a quack and not a priest. My job was science, my tools access to hospitals, tests, diagnoses and prescription pads. I had nothing else to give her.

It was only as I covered the few steps between the car and the front door that I confessed I had a less savoury admission to make. I had another reason for coming out here today. It wasn't pure concerned, professional altruism but something else: voyeurism. I had read in the local paper that Reuben Carnforth had left instructions in his will detailing where he was to be buried. Not in the churchyard's hallowed ground or the municipal cemetery but here on the farm, in Cattle Byre. And I wondered why because I knew Reuben Carnforth had been traditional in his beliefs, devout Church of England. He had mentioned Easter services to me, Harvest Festivals and Summer Fayres and I had seen him and Vera in the back pew one Christmas when I had attended the midnight service. He had been, at the very least, a Christian. So why did he not lie in the churchyard? For four months I had puzzled over this anomaly. Today I hoped I would find out why he had rejected traditional hallowed ground in favour of here. True, it was pretty, rural and near home but Reuben had been a traditionalist. He would not have rejected it without good reason. So why? I could not believe he had felt undeserving. Was there then some sin of which he and Vera had known which he believed excluded him from hallowed ground? Had the 'Help me, Doctor' been a clue? But how could I help him when I didn't know what he wanted?

I stood on the Carnforths' threshold and looked around me, at the sheds to the left where the cattle spent their winters, at the long green field which rolled towards the rim of trees. And there they stood, darkly shading the rest of the view. Even on this bright day there was a menace about those trees. I knew from my drive here that they were deceitful. They hid a sharp drop where the stone had been quarried and left rough and unguarded. This drop met the road as it curved round. It was a beautiful spot and I could understand the Carnforths' affection for this wild and beautiful place, where the only sound was the baaing of newborn lambs and the slap of the cows, chomping their

51

way through the grass. Far away I could hear a dog barking, even distant traffic, but it seemed on another planet, not this one and I returned, with a jolt, to Reuben Carnforth. I would have sworn he would have trusted the protection of the church rather than the lone wilderness of the land they had battled with all their lives.

Carry a paging device and it has the ability to intrude on even the most private thoughts. Before I'd lifted my hand to the knocker mine gave its insistent bleep. I fished it out of my pocket and flashed up the message.

Thanks for the birthday card. I'll buy you lunch at the Lazy Trout. One o'clock.

Almost an afterthought was the word on the next line, *Please,* and a capital X.

I read the message through twice before putting the pager back in my pocket and as he wasn't there I couldn't feed him the lie that after years of giving him a birthday card this one had been automatic.

It had been deliberately chosen and I knew I would turn up at the Lazy Trout at one o'clock. I felt a sudden fury at his arrogant assumption, knowing that he would have interpreted the birthday card as a ruse to see him.

Had it been? Even to myself I refused to answer the question.

I knocked on the door.

I could not be certain whether Vera was pleased to see me or not. A frozen expression masked her feelings as soon as she recognised me.

'Dr Lamont,' she said. It seemed a very formal greeting.

'How are you, Vera?'

'I'm managing.' She hesitated before offering me a cup of tea which I accepted enthusiastically.

I followed her into the high-ceilinged kitchen with its racks of drying herbs and flowers, washing steaming on a pulley. Through the open door I could see the sitting room, tidy now. Reuben's bed had been removed.

She followed my gaze and closed the door firmly. 'Yes, I miss him,' she admitted. 'It's quiet here without him. He was someone I could share things with.' Her face twisted. 'Everything with.' Her back was to me as she filled the kettle from the tap and plugged it in.

'Vera,' I said awkwardly. 'I know it's probably not my business but this is a lonely spot.'

She froze me out with a cold smile. 'You're going to try and persuade me to move, doctor?' It was a challenge.

'Into the town, Vera. Surely you can't manage the farm on your own?'

'With a bit of help,' she said. 'David Wilson comes in most mornings to help with the milking and he'll be here to dip the sheep. It's easily manageable so don't ask me to move. It isn't what I want. I don't want to leave here. I can't leave here. Whether I want to or not has nothing to do with it.'

I had expected her to add something about how much she loved Cattle's Byre but on reflection her words had held no pleasure – nothing but bitterness. And anger. Yet I felt compelled to ask, 'Is that why Reuben requested he be buried here, because he loved it?'

Her eyes were staring downwards. 'No. It wasn't. He had his own reasons.'

She handed me a cup of tea and we sat and studied one another. She spoke first. 'I'm not too grief-struck, you know. I had time to get used to it,' she said, 'Reuben's death. I knew it was coming – thanks to you.' The gratitude was awkward. 'I had time to prepare.'

Again that spectre of the cynical professor rose up to mock me. 'Was that any real help?'

'A bit,' she said, then drank deeply from her cup. 'It gave us time to talk about things. Things we'd not covered before.'

53

I thought she was referring to the rift with her son. *Listening is sometimes of more value than talking. I would learn more if I said nothing.*

She drank without dropping her eyes. 'I suppose you've been wondering why Reuben chose to be buried here.'

I flushed, caught out.

She gave me some excuse. 'Most people must imagine there was a reason.'

'I thought it must be because he was so fond of it here.' Already I knew that it was another one of my blunders.

Vera gave a dry laugh. 'It's funny what people make up,' she said, 'when they don't know the truth. They fill in bits.'

I leaned across the table. 'Then tell me,' I said. 'Tell me why you don't want to leave here. Tell me why Reuben asked to be buried here. And why did you quarrel with your son? You don't strike me as a quarrelsome woman.'

Vera pressed her lips together. A habit of keeping quiet was hard to break. Her eyes were almost hostile. 'What business is it of yours?' she demanded. 'This is family affairs. Nothing to do with a doctor.'

I put my cup down. 'Practically everything to do with your physical and mental well being is to do with your doctor,' I said. 'And you haven't got a family, Vera. You can trust me, I promise. If, on the other hand, you don't want to tell me that's OK. But I might be able to help you.'

'You won't,' she said sourly, but something in her must have melted because she started talking. 'Something happened,' she said slowly. 'It was years ago now but it affected us, me and Reuben.'

I took a deep, silent breath. 'It's still affecting you, Vera, isn't it?'

'You can't alter things from the past,' she said. 'You're stuck with them. That's the worst of it.'

More of my training was surfacing. I knew how to prompt her further. I knew all the right words to say. But my motive for wanting to know was pure curiosity. There was nothing laudable or professional about that. Just my methods. Only that.

'Sometimes the help comes from simply talking. Not necessarily changing but putting a different light on events.'

She seemed to recognise some logic in this. For a brief moment she sat and stared into space, her face mirroring her emotions as the sea reflects the weather, ripples of unhappiness followed by calm.

'Reuben asked me to help him,' I said. 'What did he mean?'

She gave a cynic's laugh. 'He had great belief in you, Doctor. He believed you could work miracles. I used to tell him that doctors were ordinary mortals, just like us, but he never quite believed it.'

'Miracles?' I frowned. 'What do you mean?'

She turned those tired eyes on me. 'It was my grand-daughter,' she said finally. 'She used to come and spend her summers with us,' she said, 'years ago. My son's child. Their only daughter. She was six years old.' She gave another of the dry laughs. 'Melanie, her name was. Melanie Toadstool, Reuben used to call her on account that she used to be fond of wearing a red dress with great big white spots on it. Wear it all the time she would, the days it wasn't in the wash.'

Now she was smiling but I had stopped. Already I felt a chill superstition that this story would cast a shadow. I might be shedding my New Year's Eve mischief but a new one was appearing. Already I knew this fairy tale had a bad ending. But my interest had been awakened and I was wondering what particular ending this story had. An accident, an illness, a tragedy?

Even I with my fertile imagination could not have guessed the terrible truth.

Vera continued in a flat, unemotional voice. 'Both my son and his wife worked. So we all thought Melanie would be much better off here, with us, through the holidays, where we could keep an eye on her far away from the smog of London, that made her chest so bad.'

She was staring at me now. 'We all thought she would be safe here. We didn't think anything would . . .'

I could not stop myself from asking. 'What did happen?'

'We never knew.'

'I don't understand.'

'She must have got up early one warm morning and wandered outside. We couldn't find her.'

'So where did . . .?'

Vera shook her head. 'You don't understand, Doctor,' she said. 'We never did find her.'

I hadn't caught up with the story. 'But what happened to her?'

'That's what I'm telling you,' Vera said patiently. 'They searched for her everywhere, right the way through the forest, in all the cowsheds. We all looked everywhere.' Again that hint of humour shone through. 'She was a great one for hiding and then springing out at people. She had such a sense of fun. We all thought she had hidden somewhere and got trapped. There's plenty of places even on a small farm like ours. They even drained the well in the back yard. But there was no sign of her.' Her face seemed to collapse like a deflated rubber mask. 'For weeks we all looked for her but it was hopeless. In the end the police had to give up. She was classed as a vanished person. We didn't know whether she'd been murdered or met with an accident and me and Reuben even wondered . . . she'd been such a pretty child. We wondered if someone had taken her for their own. Brought her up, you know. We knew that if she returned anywhere it would be here. We couldn't think that she might be dead.' She glanced around the kitchen. 'Truth was we'd had enough of farming years ago but every time we came close to leaving we'd think the same thing. What if she came back and there were strangers here?'

'But surely,' I objected, 'this entire episode was years ago.'

'Ten.'

'Then Melanie would now be sixteen. She can't still be . . .'

Her knuckles were bone-white as they still gripped her coffee mug. 'Sense and reason might tell you that. The love we felt for that little girl had nothing to do with either. We'd keep imagining things, that she'd pop out from behind a tree or something. You have to understand. She was that sort of a child. Unexpected. You just never knew with her.'

'Not after ten years,' I said, and Vera gave a low sigh.

'Not after ten years. But Reuben and I have always felt she isn't so very far away.'

'So that's why . . .?'

And Vera nodded. 'She'd find Reuben.'

'I'm so sorry,' I said, and pushed my hand towards hers. She could have taken it but there was something else. She was studying the grain on the table in a concerted effort not to meet my eyes. 'There was something else, Doctor.' Her voice was brittle now. Brittle as thin glass. 'There was worse.'

I couldn't imagine.

'Tongues started wagging. Some people said . . . they said . . . the police tried to say that Reuben had been interfering with her.'

I shook my head hard. 'Oh no, Vera. No.'

'We couldn't prove it either way,' she said. 'Because they never found her they never knew what happened. They had nothing to go on, you see. But we knew while there was all this uncertainty we wouldn't be welcome back in the town. So we stayed,' she finished simply. At least Reuben knew I trusted him. I knew the truth. He loved our little girl. But there was nothing abnormal in his love. It was healthy, good love. Natural too.'

'Did the police have nothing to go on?'

'Oh they found her dress, torn, not so far away.' A spasm crossed her face. 'I suppose they've still got it somewhere.

Just in case . . .' For a moment she was unable to continue.

I waited.

'They pulled a few people in for questioning but it never led anywhere. You see this is a quiet place. Melanie went out very early that morning. Even we were asleep and we rise at half five. There was no one around to watch her.'

Even then I knew the truth. That someone *had* been around to watch her. Someone knew exactly what had happened to the child. And that someone knew where she was now.

And I was disturbed by the powerful image of the child in a red and white spotted dress, running across a field. I knew this vision would haunt me for the months ahead.

'If I'd been the fanciful sort,' Vera was saying, 'I'd have thought she really had been turned into a toadstool. There's plenty out there, in the trees. One more no one would notice.'

'And your son?'

'Believed the worst.' She must have seen my face because she quickly added, 'Oh, not about Reuben. Not even he could believe that about his own father. He held us responsible for everything else but not that. All the same I have heard nothing from him since then. Not a single word. I have heard they have another child. I suppose you can't blame them for not wanting to bring it here. Maybe they think-' She was struggling to keep the tears back. 'Reuben and I wanted to drive down to London. We wanted to look at her, to see if she looked like our Melanie. But we never did. We wondered.' Her eyes wandered past me to the empty sitting room. 'Nights we'd sit down and wonder.'

'Does your son know his father's dead?'

'I wrote when he was ill. I wrote again after Reuben died, telling him when the funeral was. I heard nothing. I'm surprised no one mentioned it to you.'

'I suppose if it was just gossip . . .' I said lamely.

She stood up. 'You must want to see, Doctor.' There was a disturbing cognisance behind her eyes as though she could read the motive that lay behind my professional talk. 'I'll take you there.'

Neither of us spoke as we tramped across the field, through a herd of cows, and approached the tree-line and a long mound of freshly turned earth marked with a simple wooden cross bearing the name Reuben Carnforth, the date and the year. There was an inscription, unusual on most tombstones, logical on this.

Seek and Ye Shall Find.

But he hadn't. Had he? I glanced around and had a sudden clarity of vision.

'Did he specify this precise spot?'

Vera nodded.

There was a rotting tree stump beside a post. Perhaps, ten years ago, a child might have used it to climb before jumping off the other side.

Had Reuben known this? By instinct? Or had he seen her?

Vera was staring down at the grave, her fists clenched. 'I have to know,' she said. 'I cannot leave this life not knowing, never knowing. It's eating me up like a cancer. While I had Reuben it was at least bearable, just. We both could keep her alive by remembering her. And I knew if she was found that Reuben and I could go to London, to our son and make our peace. But it's too late for him now. And one day it'll be too late for me too. I just can't stand that thought.'

She was gripping the top rail of the fence as she spoke, facing not the house but the edge of the trees. 'They know,' she said. 'Bloody things. Sometimes I think I hate them. It's as though they grow to hide things. Damned trees,' she said again and I knew she must have stood here and scanned the trees a thousand times before, through hot summers and chill winters, soaking autumns and bright green springs, and on New Year's Eve too, longing for the child to pop out from behind one of the trees. Except she never did. Melanie had remained hidden. And now, surely, it must be too late. She must be dead.

I didn't mention the steep drop to the road. Vera must know about it and that possibility had surely been explored. I followed Vera back to the farm, leaving her at the door.

'I'll come again,' I said.

'If you like.' At the door she paused, still scanning the skirt of trees. 'If only Reuben was right and Doctors really did have some special powers. If only by some miracle you really could find out what had happened to her.' She gave an abstracted smile. 'Silly, isn't it, Doctor, the way we clutch at straws? Then she closed the door firmly behind her.

I felt altered all the way back down to the town. It was as though the story of the missing child had wrought a catharsis.

She felt like my responsibility.

Everywhere looked different, the cliff, clearly visible from the road, jagged and dangerous to a child, the causeway, the Heron Pool, where it was easy to slip through the reeds, easy to fall and be swallowed up in the still water. And the winding lane seemed menacingly remote and deserted. As I drove through the trees I kept turning my head quickly as though I might catch a glimpse of the child even though I knew it was not possible. Maybe it was the ridiculous name by which her grandparents had called her but she didn't seem a real kid, like Rosie. Rather she was a wraith, something that could still jump out from behind a tree even though she had vanished ten years before. In fact the child's presence was so strong that I tilted my rear view mirror sure I would catch sight of her. Even in the water I searched for her reflection and when a wood pigeon burst through the trees my heart skipped a couple of beats. The cloudburst seemed to echo the threat and I switched my windscreen wipers and lights on. The sun had vanished. I was glad to return to town and civilisation.

The Lazy Trout was an old stamping ground of ours, a beamed black and white pub with roaring fires and a menu that would convert an anorexic. Robin and I had patronised it when I had first joined the practice seven years ago and our lively, two-year-old toddler had made us the pariahs of most civilised restaurants.

It was a clever choice of Robin's, calculated to evoke memories of happier times. Even sliding the Carlton next to the black Mercedes conjured up some vivid memories. When we had first come here I had been enthused by my vision of general practice, something to do with generous government funding plus a certain youthful optimism. Robin had swum along with my dream, like the lazy trout of the pub. Yet, almost unnoticed by me, his accountancy business had also flourished. Whatever virtues he had – charm, a head for figures, business sense – they had all combined to make him successful.

And me?

I got threatened by a druggie because I wouldn't give him what he wanted and still had to tumble out of bed in response to my patients' sometimes unreasonable demands. Times had changed. I locked my car door, skirted a deep puddle and entered the pub.

Inside there was the wonderful scent of bacon frying combined with some ancient muck from farmers' wellies. This was not a pub to stand on ceremony, not some 'country pub' dreamed up by the brewers to hoodwink townies but a working pub that catered for locals and merely tolerated tourists.

The lounge bar was kept permanently darkened by tiny windows and a low, beamed ceiling on which Robin had hit his head more than once. In the corner stood wooden

Edwardian bar skittles beneath a bowed, glass case containing a stuffed trout. Lazy this one certainly was.

I picked Robin out immediately, leaning against the bar, chatting to some of the locals. It was one of his most dubious charms that although throughout our married life I had invariably waited for him on any social occasion, when on a date he was unfailingly punctual.

His mistresses had fared better than his wife. But, I considered with amusement, now that I was disengaging myself from being his wife was I elevated to the position of mistress? Was this a surreptitious date? Did Janina know he was meeting me?

I found the thought amusing and gave Robin a warmer smile than I had planned. The idea of Robin sneaking off to meet me was attractive. I studied the blunt, good humoured face before standing on tip toes and kissing him on the cheek. He felt the same, slightly scratchy, aftershave tangy but faint. Collar crisp, scent of spray starch.

I had trouble disliking him. No trouble hating her.

He followed me to a table, banged his head on the beam and grinned at me without a trace of self-consciousness. 'Hi, Harry,' Hurtfully his voice was as warm as though he was addressing his favourite sister. With a sinking heart I realised what was missing from it. Lust. That had been the missing factor.

I responded in kind and, to my credit, without rancour. 'Hello.' I hoped he couldn't hear the struggle in my greeting. As I settled warily across the table from him I wondered. Did his eyes have to be such a bright, hurtful blue?

He dropped back into the chair; stretching out his long legs. He began politely enough with thanks for the birthday card before he said, 'You're looking rough.'

'I wish I could return the insult.'

He brushed my spiky compliment aside. 'I mean it, Harry. Is something wrong?' That he could ask such a question.

'Nothing apart from my marriage breaking up and my daughter missing her father.'

His eyes flickered. 'I've been busy.'

It was a pathetic excuse. 'At weekends?'

'How about a drink?' he said quickly.

'Fine.' It was wonderful how he thought he could distract me from my purpose but I could play games too. 'White wine, please.'

I was gratified to see Robin's eyes widen. 'You aren't turning to drink, are you? You never drink in the day. It gives you a headache.'

I leaned forward. 'I would like a drink and I don't seem to get headaches these days.'

'Touché,' he said and ambled towards the bar.

He was served quickly and came straight back again, flipping a menu across the table.

'So Happy Birthday,' I said, raising my glass. 'And is it happy?'

'So . . . so . . . Obviously I worry about you and Rosie.'

Even from my psychopathic husband it was an obvious lie. However, I should have worked the whole thing out before I came. Robin was playing another part, concerned ex-husband, absent father.

He grinned and ran his fingers through his hair. It flopped straight back over his eyebrows as it had been cut to do. 'So when I got your birthday card, well, it seemed an ideal opportunity to …'

'Renew old friendships?'

His confidence was only marginally displaced. 'We're a bit more than an old friendship, Harriet.'

'The birthday card was pure habit,' I said. 'It's hard to let May the eighteenth go by without marking it somehow. And I really am fine, in spite of the way I look.'

Robin was watching me with a faintly pitying look. 'Don't be proud, Harry,' he said. 'We were married for ten years – remember?'

'And now we're getting divorced.'

He gave a heartfelt sigh of regret. 'You seem a bit on edge,' he said.

I began telling him then about the missing child, Vera Carnforth, and Reuben's burial site. 'I can't believe that he didn't tell me,' I said. 'Such a huge life event, his own granddaughter's abduction and he didn't confide in me. He said nothing. He never even mentioned it. Apart from the last plea.'

Robin was, for once, unusually perceptive. 'But you didn't confide in him, did you?'

'What do you mean?'

'I'm sure I remember you telling me,' he said, 'round about Christmas time, that his wife was insisting he wasn't told he had cancer.'

'That's right,' I said, 'but I'm surprised you remembered.'

'Mmm.' He smiled. 'Maybe sometimes you misjudge me.'

I said nothing.

'Perhaps,' he said, 'if you'd been straighter with him he might have felt able to unload his problem.'

For my husband this was a searingly perceptive remark.

The food arrived then and for minutes our mouths were too busy even to argue. I had known he would go for the fillet steak. Red blooded, carnivorous male – what else? I finished my meal first, pushed my plate back and moved my head, catching a faint tang of orange scented perfume.

He spoke first. 'So tell me more about this missing child.'

'Her name was Melanie,' I said sharply. 'She vanished very early one summer's morning, ten years ago, and was never seen again. She was ten years old, Robin, just a little older than our daughter.'

Memories of Melanie Carnforth stayed with me over the next month. I could never quite erase her from my mind. At night I would close my eyes and see her, as a red and white toadstool with a laughing face, peeping from behind trees, a child wandering across the field on a sunny morning. My dreams were filled with visions of her walking towards the dark edge of the Carnforths' field. And the more I tried to warn her the worse it was. I could not speak. My mouth was too dry, my tongue too firmly glued to the roof of my mouth.

The dream always ended in exactly the same way. The child reached the fence. And there was Reuben's mound of red-brown earth. She stopped and stroked it before climbing the rotting tree stump. For some reason I could always see a massive bracket fungus sticking out of the side. And yet I did not recall having noticed one there. Maybe it was the natural link between the toadstool colours of the child's dress and another fungus. I must check next time I wandered to the edge of the field.

The child climbed the tree stump, stood for a while and jumped . . . and before my eyes she vanished. But I could still hear her laughing when I woke in a cold sweat.

I sat up. In my anxiety to protect Rosie I was transferring the threat to her.

Once or twice I even padded into her room to check her. The second time she woke.

'Mum?'

'It's OK.' I felt a fool. 'Really, Rosie, it's OK.'

There was another aspect to the dreams: the child's face as she touched the mound where her grandfather lay. There was a bleakness about it that I was tempted to inter-pret as acceptance. When Vera had first told me about the police insinuations I had rejected them. Now I was not so confident. Like Vera I wished the case had been solved ten years ago and someone charged, found guilty and sentenced. Then there would be no clouds of suspicion. Reuben would have lain in the haven of the churchyard with a headstone that paid some tribute to a brave life and maybe, just maybe, Vera and her son could then have been reconciled. The whole thing was so incomplete scars were still forming ten years later.

It seemed that Anthony Pritchard had decided he should attend the surgery once a month. Always to see me, always to have his blood pressure checked. And each time I knew he was inching closer to me, trying to break down the doctor/patient barrier. He considered me his friend, his dear friend.

'Harriet,' he said on his June visit. 'I have to say I think you're a wonderful doctor.'

'Just doing my job, *Mr* Pritchard.'

'Oh come on,' he said, 'do start calling me Anthony. We know each other well now.'

I'd had enough. 'Mr Pritchard,' I said. 'It doesn't do for doctors and patients to call each other by their Christian names. The relationship is a formal one.' I wanted to wound him. 'I get paid an annual retainer for looking after you. This isn't really a friendship.'

'Are you telling me, *Harriet,* that you never treat your friends?'

I thought of Ruth, undoubtedly my own patient. But the friendship had come first. She had transferred to my list after disagreeing with her previous doctor.

'I try not to treat my friends, Mr Pritchard,' I said. 'As I said, the doctor/patient relationship works better if it is kept on a formal footing.'

'You are my doctor. I like you being my doctor. It gives me a warm feeling.' He gave something which I imagined was meant to be a conspiratorial smile. 'It's only that I think of you as my friend too.'

'Mr Pritchard.' I tried again. 'You don't need to see a doctor on a monthly basis. We have a very good nurse who is perfectly capable of monitoring your blood pressure without you even needing to see me.'

'I know,' he said, smiling, 'but I like to come. To tell you the truth I enjoy visiting you.' His voice was soft, with a Northern accent, full of insinuation. He leaned forward, pushed his glasses up his nose with a fat forefinger. 'I would miss our monthly chats, Harriet,' he said, 'so much that I am reluctant to discontinue them. I think there's something somewhere about guaranteed access to a medical opinion. I must say I rest easier in my bed having that assurance.'

And I knew as he left that he had got the upper hand.

The room was stuffy. I badly needed to breathe untainted air. I scrambled out of my chair, shot out of the door; straight into Neil Anderson's arms.

'Good gracious, Harriet,' he said. 'what on earth's the matter?'

Out of the corner of my eye I saw Danny Small follow Pritchard out through the surgery door.

'That man,' I said and breathed in the scent of soap gratefully. There was something clean, fragrant, wholesome about Neil.

He followed my glance. 'Who?'

'Pritchard.' My heart rate was beginning to slow down. 'He keeps coming in for a monthly blood pressure check.'

Neil laughed. 'I've got loads of people who think they'll die without it, Harry. Just get him to come in and see Miriam. She's good at handling awkward customers.'

I was stung. 'And I'm not?'

Neil touched my shoulder 'Obviously not, Harriet,' he said gravely. 'Not if he can rattle you as badly as all that.'

'I keep telling him to come in and see the nurse. Unfortunately he doesn't take a blind bit of notice.'

'Well it's just a quick BP check,' he said. 'Doesn't take up much of your time.'

'It isn't the time,' I said. 'It's the insinuations.'

Neil's grip on my shoulder tightened. 'What, that middle-aged man, making suggestions? Surely you can deal with that?'

I was sliding down in his estimation. 'They aren't exactly suggestions,' I said.

'So what are they?' Neil was running out of patience.

'He just gets too close,' I said. 'Let's just put it like that.'

Neil smiled and moved away. 'Well, they aren't a troublesome family,' he said. 'I've never done a visit to their place and neither have you although I've been here for fifteen years. Harriet,' he said, 'these are the patients we want to keep.' Neil's eyes wandered back towards the door. Danny Small was lighting up in the path of any patient who wanted to enter the surgery. 'That's the sort we need to get rid of, Harriet, buggers like that,' he said viciously. 'Now if you'll excuse me I've got visits to do.'

We had a practice agreement that no patient was to be crossed off our list without good reason and the consent of all three partners. I did not dare bring up the subject again. After all, one appointment, in the safety of the surgery, lasting ten minutes, once a month. Surely I could cope with that?

Six months after Robin had left I decided the time was ripe to clear out every last vestige of his existence. I knew that it was all over between us and there was no going back. But Rosie hadn't accepted it and I still found her getting Robin's favourite breakfast cereal out occasionally in the mornings as though she was willing him to turn up for it.

It was hot. I had the windows open, the radio tuned to loud pop music, an iced tea in my hand. I showered, pulled on some shorts and an old, navy T-shirt and armed myself with black plastic bin liners before starting in the kitchen, fumbling right to the back of the food cupboard, searching for signs of Robin.

Then I went upstairs and winkled out a couple of pairs of worn boxer shorts, socks with holes, shirts with missing buttons, a red silk cumberbund and some dreadfully smelly aftershave. I stuffed the lot in another black plastic bin liner and left it all for the dustbin men to find when they came on Monday. Lastly I came to his miniature chest of drawers, the mahogany reproduction that stood at what I still thought of as his side of the bed.

We all have our secrets.

Right at the bottom I found a little faded green shoe box which I had never seen before. He must have kept it well hidden for years. It was not big enough to contain Robin's size tens. I handled it curiously. This box was only big enough to have contained children's shoes. Surely he hadn't kept an old box of Rosie's shoes? He had been the least sentimental of fathers. But the side of the box did pronounce size fourteens, children's Startrite sandals. So who else's could they be? I put my hand on the lid with the feeling I was about to discover something significant about Robin. Perhaps, after all, he had had some deep, sentimental regard for his daughter. Maybe I had misjudged him. I lifted the lid and rested it on the bed only to feel the habitual disappointment. It had nothing to do with Rosie. This was Robin's secret hoard of Robin, a magpie collection of childhood treasures, a couple of vintage matchbox toys, a London taxi, a small red bus, a couple of Thunderbird models. Of course. I had used the wrong yardstick. To Robin only Robin was important – not his daughter.

And yet. I picked up the London bus with its Marmite sign on the side. The boyish toys gave me another side to Robin, a side that right now I did not want to dwell on, the small, plump, vulnerable boy I had seen in faded photographs proudly displayed by a mother whose husband, I had always suspected, had abandoned her when he had realised her obsession with her son would be exclusive and all absorbing. Such mothers bred such sons.

I was about to replace the lid when I noticed a black-bordered envelope, right at the bottom. It surprised me. It was so out of character; sombre and old-fashioned, yellowed, dog-eared and depressing. Surely not a death notice? Robin would not keep such things. He had a horror of illness and mortality, avoiding people's funerals as though he could catch death itself. He never visited anyone when they were sick. He had only come to see me in hospital after Rosie's birth under duress from his mother. And when I had lost my second baby he had not visited me at all, making one limp excuse after another. And I had understood. His perception of me had subtly altered. He had seen me as imperfect, unhealthy. I suppose under the circumstances it was strange that he had married a doctor. I made my living out of sickness, disease, ill health. I sat back on my heels, my mouth dropping open at this strange thought. Why had Robin married me?

I did not need to peer in the mirror to know it had not been for my looks. I suppose it was then that I worked it out, like some complicated physics formula. He had regarded me as a talisman against disease. Again Robin had not let me down. Robin had married me because Robin was concerned about Robin. So he had married a doctor. As I was superstitious enough to buy candles throughout the summer to ward off winter power cuts so Robin had been superstitious enough to marry me. It was a stunning realisation. And this had masqueraded as love. As I fingered the stiff envelope I wondered how this fitted into the concept. Why had he kept this? An invitation to a funeral. It was this which made no sense. Not our impending divorce. That had been inevitable from the beginning. I slipped the card out. The date, 1965, the month, November, the name, Lorna Garbett, aged seventy-five years. I puzzled over it and remembered that Garbett had been his mother's maiden name. I could remember her telling me quite proudly that she had intended giving Robin the surname Garbett-Lamont. But his father had blocked the idea. I had often thought that I would have liked Robin's father a lot more than his mother. Unfortunately I had never met him.

So Lorna Garbett would have been Robin's maternal grandmother. I studied the black-bordered card for a while, trying to glean information from it and wondering what sort of woman she had been for Robin to have kept this macabre reminder of her death.

I could never remember seeing a photograph of her. Not here nor in his mother's house. So why keep this? In 1965 Robin would have been a little boy of just four years old with, surely, a horror of death. I slipped the card back in the envelope and replaced the lid of the box, shutting out memories and questions, but I did not throw it away. I stuck the box on top of the wardrobe, out of sight, and sat still for a while, my mind drifting along possibilities. Perhaps this was part of the explanation of Robin's fear of death. Had the old woman held such influence over him? At such a tender age? Or had it been love? I found myself fascinated by the puzzle. Why had he kept the funeral card?

I don't know how long I sat there. Probably I would have stayed a lot longer but I gradually became aware of the telephone ringing. I know I felt glad of the diversion, even gladder that it was Ruth, suggesting we meet for lunch. I had hardly seen her since the New Year's Eve party. True – we were both professional women, busy, with little time to spare, but her silence had hurt and secretly I had agonised over the idea that she and Arthur had kept up the friendship with Robin at the expense of our own relationship.

We arranged to meet on the following Wednesday, at a small wine bar in the centre of town on the hottest day yet of that year. There was an added spring in people's step as they sweltered around the streets, enjoying the sunshine, licking ice creams and downing drinks. Unwilling to make a fruitless search for a space I parked in one of the emptier, out of town car parks, which meant a stiff climb up a narrow cobbled street towards the bistro.

The shops were filled with summer clothes, Tshirts, espadrilles, bikinis and swimsuits together with strappy dresses and shorts. The antique shop threw out the sparkle of freshly polished furniture and bright, washed ornaments. There was even a nineteen twenties picnic basket complete with crystal wine glasses and flowered bone china set out on a checked tablecloth. Very imaginative. Next door was a children's outfitters. I lingered for a while, admiring the pretty dresses, tastefully set out with buckets and spades, mock sandcastles and plastic inflatable ducks and I yearned for the time when Rosie would have worn such feminine fripperies, in the days before she had defected to saggy T-shirts and leggings. I glanced at my watch and moved on.

Even the butcher's shop was making an effort to match the hot weather with trussed chickens, barbecued chicken breasts, and long lamb kebabs together with pieces of fillet steak begging for charcoal. I spotted the butcher near the back of the shop, chopping up meat for a customer; and carried on walking with an uncomfortable feeling that I had seen something to disturb me. It lasted all the way up the hill until I reached the bow-fronted windows of the bistro and pushed open the door.

It was almost empty inside, apart from a table of girls who looked as though they were celebrating something. A birthday, leaving work, a wedding, a baby? Ruth was propping up the bar, sipping a drink. She put the glass down heavily and gave me a long, lugubrious look before flinging her arms around me. 'Harry,' she said. 'I'm so sorry. It was a rotten start to the New Year.'

A wave of bitterness swamped me and again I was glad that the Carnforths had called me out that night and saved me from both my friends' sympathy and my own embarrassment. But summoning the Carnforths back into my mind evoked the tinge of unease. It was a little more awareness. In one of the shop windows I had seen something that had reminded me of Melanie. Troubled, I fished around at the back of my mind, mentally walking back down the hill.

Not the butcher's? A swift vision of the rows of red meat, trussed chickens, the kebabs. Butcher standing in striped apron, long knife in his hand. Not there.

I would know it when I found it.

My mind moved backwards to the children's outfitters, plaster model children, buckets and spades, sandcastles, paper flags and plastic ducks, a woman in a red dress serving someone. But again I failed to find the cause for my feeling of discomfort. It had not been there.

So back to the antiques shop? The most unlikely candidate, surely? But straight away the hammering was there, right at the back of my mind. Shining objects, gleaming furniture, china, pictures . . .

'Back to the present.' Ruth was staring at me. 'You look as though you've seen a ghost. Harriet, whatever's the matter?'

I tried really hard to laugh it off but Ruth wasn't buying. 'Come on, Harry,' she said. 'We're friends enough for you to confide in me.'

'I think I must have spotted something,' I said, 'in one of the shops. It reminded me of a story I heard recently.'

'Well, it must have upset you.'

'Yes it did,' I said. 'More than I realised.'

'So what was it?'

'That's the trouble,' I said. 'I don't know what it was. I only know it registered at the time.'

'I meant what was the story?'

'Ruth,' I said abruptly, 'how long have you lived in Larkdale?'

She gave one of her loud, throaty laughs. 'More years than I care to remember.' I waited. 'About twenty years,' she said. 'I think it was 1978 when we came here. I started as deputy head practically fresh from university.'

'Do you remember a little girl going missing, about ten years ago?'

She frowned. 'Yes,' she said. 'I do, vaguely. A little kid of about six. Wasn't she staying with her grandparents? Weren't they farmers?'

'They're patients of mine,' I said. 'At least the grandfather was.'

'Was?'

'He died early this year but the grandmother is still living in the same place.'

'Somewhere up in the forest, wasn't it? A farm?'

I nodded. 'More of a smallholding.' Ruth waited. At the time,' I said, 'what did you think happened to the child?'

She wrinkled her nose up. 'Well, at first everyone thought she'd simply wandered off. She was only little and the forest is enormous. Goes on for miles. Besides. You know there's a quarry up there. It's quite steep. She could easily have fallen.'

'And later,' I asked. 'When they failed to find her? What did you think then?'

'Well, I think after a week or so most people discounted the possibility that she had simply fallen. I mean they would have found her – wouldn't they?'

I nodded. 'So?'

'It seemed more likely that someone had abducted and murdered her.'

'Who?'

'Lots of people were dragged in for questioning. But no one was ever charged. Quite honestly,' Ruth said, 'I always thought they had the right man all the time. Some creepy character who'd been out walking his dog. At five o'clock in the morning? They questioned him but released him. No evidence.' Her voice was crisply condemning.

'Who was it?'

Ruth laughed. 'I can't remember his name, Harry. It was all a long time ago. You know how it is, ten-day wonders. It was rather horrible though, dragging the pools and checking through undergrowth. Arthur helped look for her.' She smiled. 'They gave him a whistle in case he found anything. I mean – Arthur.' She looked curiously at me. 'But I still can't see why you're even interested. It was ages before you came here. Surely even the grandparents got over it eventually?'

'Not really. Vera Carnforth told me,' I said cautiously, 'that the police even questioned Reuben about . . .'

Ruth was quick to grasp my meaning. 'Good gracious. Nobody believed that for a minute. He was in bed with his wife when the child went missing.'

'She was his alibi then?'

'I suppose so. But no one ever really thought it was him.'

'He thought they did. And so did his wife. And I suppose while the disappearance is unsolved they can't prove otherwise. And of course now he's dead. He'll never know. His wife is anxious to clear his name and she wants to know what happened to the child.'

Ruth's face changed. 'Oh,' she said. 'Poor thing to live under such suspicion.'

I nodded. 'He was a decent man, Ruth. I know it.'

'I don't see what it's got to do with you, Harriet. Surely it's a job for the police. Not a family doctor.'

'I'm not appointing myself chief investigator.' I blurted it out then. 'On New Year's Eve it was to the Carnforths' farm that I was called. Reuben was dying.' A vision of the bony fingers gave me sudden pain. 'He asked me to help him. Naturally I thought he meant for me to cure his illness. But it wasn't that. Later his wife told me he had blind faith that I could somehow help trace what had happened to his granddaughter.'

'That's silly.'

75

'Of course it is,' I said, 'but silly or not I can't stop thinking about it. And now today something's made me even more aware of the little girl.'

She leaned forward. 'What?'

'I don't know.'

'A toy shop? Did you pass a toy shop, Harry?'

'No.'

'Some kiddies' clothes, then?'

I frowned. 'There was but I don't think it was in there. They had all sorts of summer dresses, ducks and plastic buckets and things.'

'Well, she disappeared on a hot day in the middle of summer; didn't she? In a red dress?'

Melanie Toadstool.

'A red dress with white spots.'

Ruth looked even more concerned. 'I can see you really are interested.'

I nodded. 'I'll take another look on the way back.'

'Then I hope you find it,' she said. 'Because otherwise it will lie at the back of your mind and haunt you.'

'It is,' I said cautiously.

She gave me one of her warm smiles. Almost motherly. 'This has really bothered you, hasn't it?'

I nodded. 'I've been having dreams about it.'

'Why? Simply because he was your patient?'

'Maybe it's not just Reuben's charge,' I said. 'It's Rosie. Since Robin went I've felt more vulnerable, more responsible for her.'

'Yes, poor Rosie.'

'She's growing up very fast,' I said.

We chose our meal, sat back and made conversation, about Ruth's work and the Ofsted schools inspectors, about my current position with the health service, then she asked about Rosie which gave me the opportunity to confide in her things I had not told anyone, how she sometimes wet the bed, how her new friends seemed different from her old ones, how my placid little daughter sometimes produced language that would have shocked the BBC.

'Have you told Robin?'

'He isn't interested in her any more.'

'Oh dear.' Ruth gave a long sigh.

By the time we had eaten the conversation seemed to run out and instinctively I knew that Ruth had asked me here for a purpose and not out of coincidence. My best friend and it had taken her the best part of an hour to pluck up the courage to ask me.

'Harriet,' she began doggedly. 'I wanted to ask you something. It's medical,' she warned, 'but I didn't want to come to the surgery. I felt too embarrassed.'

I picked up my coffee cup. 'So fire away,' I said. 'That's what friends are for.'

Her face was flushed scarlet.

I put the cup back in the saucer and waited. Ruth was sitting facing the light so I could see her face very clearly. She was wearing more make-up than usual and it filled the deep creases around her eyes, the furrows between her eyebrows, the channels carved between her nose and mouth. I suddenly realised that Ruth was more colourful than she used to be. But, like the autumn, the colour announced her growing years instead of disguising them.

Without warning her eyes filled. Annoyed, she gave a sniff. 'Oh, bugger,' she said, and gave a second sniff noisy enough to have earned any of her pupils a telling off. The water level in her eyes dropped. 'I want a baby,' she said simply. 'I know I'm forty-six years old. I know I've always said I didn't want children. I know all that,' she finished defiantly.

I was stunned. 'But you've always said . . .'

'I know,' she continued, 'the HRT.' She made another attempt at a smile. 'I'm probably halfway through the menopause already but I want a child. I want one terribly badly.'

77

I gawped at her. 'But . . .'

'Of my own,' she said fiercely. 'It hit me a couple of weeks ago. I watch the children move through the school. But they leave, Harry. They leave. They are at the school for up to seven years and most of them go without a backwards glance. They go home to their mothers and fathers and I am left with the empty school. I have nothing of my own.'

She cupped her chin in her hand. 'I went in over the half term,' she said, 'and had a really good look around. All the stuff was still on the walls. One or two of the kids had left their coats behind.' She gave me a humorous glance. 'There was a frightful stink of old trainers and stale sports equipment but there wasn't a single human being there.' She stopped speaking for a moment and stared straight past me, in a world of her own. 'It was so lonely, almost ghost-like. All those children vanishing into the world without trace.'

I started. The feeling of something just behind me was as strong as the day I had first heard about Melanie. Luckily Ruth hadn't noticed my lapse of concentration. She was still talking.

'It struck me then in that empty, silent school. It was like home.'

'Home? Ruth. Your home isn't anything like that.'

'No?' She challenged me. 'How would you know?'

She was wrecking all my delusions. 'But you and Arthur are happy together, just yourselves.'

Her eyebrows peaked in the middle. 'Yes?'

'But I always thought . . .' I couldn't go on blundering through these boundaries of delusion and as usual when in a dilemma I hid behind the shield of medicine. 'Do you know what you're asking?'

'I think I've an idea.'

'Even being generous I'd say your chances are slim.' I paused. 'Why now when it's so much more difficult? If you had maternal feelings why wait until now?'

'Because I didn't know.' She leaned forward. 'I've been a headmistress for fifteen years,' she said bitterly. 'I became a teacher because I really like children and I enjoy teaching them. Not just teaching them. Being with them.' Ruth's hand was on my arm. 'Just tell me, Harry,' she said tensely, 'is it possible? Am I capable of bearing a child?'

'Theoretically,' I said in a professional, cautious voice, 'if you have regular periods and are ovulating regularly there should be no problem.'

'But?'

'Let's get down to basics, Ruth.'

She looked embarrassed. 'I shouldn't have dragged you out for lunch only to spring this on you.'

'It's OK.' I watched the waiter pour a second coffee and made a joke of it. 'Yearning for a family does happen,' I said, 'especially with middle-aged, nulliparous professional women.'

She burst out laughing. 'Nulliparous,' she said. 'Harry, are you insulting me?'

I joined her laughing, at long last feeling the desired good. This was nothing to do with bereavement, sickness or disease. This was an appeal to aid life itself. Surely that was at the heart of our profession? Not illness, suffering, death? Life. I wanted more than anything to help her. 'Have you ever been pregnant?'

'No.' She gave a frank smile. 'Not even a tucked-away teenage abortion to confess to.'

'Hmm.'

'Don't give me one of your "Hmms",' she said, her face still tense. 'What are you going to do for me?'

'We'll start with some serum hormone levels,' I said. 'And I need to take a proper history. The chances aren't particularly good but it is possible – theoretically.'

She stood up then and hugged me. 'Thank you, Harry, thank you enormously.'

'But Ruth,' I said awkwardly, 'it isn't just conceiving. That's tricky enough. It's hanging on to the pregnancy. And you have a much greater chance of having a baby born with some sort of defect.'

'I know that,' she said, her chin firm and square. 'Arthur and I have discussed all this.' 'Then first,' I said, 'you have to stop the HRT. And the best of luck.'

And so my patients twirled a grotesque jig around me, Pritchard, Danny Small, Vera Carnforth. And now Ruth had joined them. I was in the centre, part yet not part of the slow dance. And I did not know which one to face.

We left the café soon after and went our separate ways, me to wander back down the narrow cobbled street which returned me to the car park, leaving behind the crowds of the town. It was quiet yet I dawdled. There was no hurry. Rosie was playing with a friend all afternoon. I could pick her up at any time. And so I found myself in front of the three shops again, gazing into the butcher's shop window, focusing on every single object in turn. It was with a sick feeling of relief that I recognised no quickening of my pulse or that unhappy, uncomfortable feeling. It was not here in the bloody lumps of meat or the butcher's knife that I had picked up my disquiet. I moved on.

Surely Ruth was right. It must be here? The splash of colour in the children's clothes shop was bold and cheerful. The clothes were expensive and old-fashioned, plaster models playing on the beach. A summer scene and it had been in the summer on just such a hot day, that the child had vanished. I stared into the window for ages, willing it to tell me what had given me such an uneasy feeling. But it didn't come back.

I saw nothing but the beach scene, the plaster models, the plastic ducks, the sandcastles. It was not here either.

So, puzzled, I returned to the antique shop. But it seemed unlikely. At first I saw nothing but the Edwardian picnic set, the polished writing boxes, a coffer with carved legs displaying a jumble of porcelain. It was as my eyes wandered towards the back of the shop that I felt a bang of recognition. I knew. It was on the far wall, not part of the window display at all. It was surprising I had noticed it, less surprising that it had been my subconscious which had absorbed it enough to plague my mind during lunch. It was a 1920s print, poor quality, in an oak frame and showed a girl sitting with her arms around a fly agaric, the red and white spotted toadstool so beloved of fairy illustrators. It was a strange combination. A child embracing a poisonous fungus? I stared at it for a long time, shielding my eyes against the glare of the sun reflected in the shop window and stupidly I convinced myself that there was a connection between the disappearance of a little girl ten years ago and the cheap, mass produced picture.

Surely the title of the print must be 'The Enigma of Melanie Toadstool'?

I tried the door of the shop. Frustratingly it was closed. Today was the traditional early closing day for Larkdale. But so few shopkeepers actually put the shutters up I had forgotten the town still had such a thing. Only quiet shops in empty backstreets closed on a Wednesday. I turned away and headed back to the car. It was gone three.

I had left my car facing forwards between two empty spaces, not being one of those who fanatically reverses into parking areas. Though the car park was still almost empty the space next to mine had been filled by a dark blue Lada. But the driver had parked too close for me to open my door. I glanced around, annoyed. It was so unnecessary. The bloody car park was empty because the steep climb over cobbles made it an unpopular place from which to shop, especially on such a hot day, tricky to use a pushchair, hazardous for the elderly, too far for the lazy. Most people would rather pay the extra charge and chance the town car parks than climb the hill. I stared at the two cars for a moment, muttering. Then I squeezed between them. I even managed to insert my key in the car door but I could only open it a fraction. There was no chance of me climbing in that way, thin though I was. And once I had got in the car it would take a steady hand on the wheel to pull away without marking the Lada. Oh well, it would serve him right if I scraped his side. I didn't care about his car. Mine was a different matter I didn't want a scratch or a dent. For now I would have to clamber in through the passenger side.

But even here there was a problem. Like many people who habitually drove alone my passenger seat was cluttered with papers, sets of notes, my Gladstone bag and a town map. There was also a yellow plastic box in which I discarded used syringes and broken glass ampoules. I didn't fancy climbing over it. Still furious, I rounded my car and peered inside the blue Lada. It was an old car scruffy and muck-splattered. The driver was either a farmer or someone who habitually drove through the country. That made me even more intrigued. Country people usually kept their distance. It was the townies who crowded one, people who were chronically used to having too little space, people from small rooms and overcrowded dwellings. This country person had strange manners.

Maybe he would return. I glanced around me but the car park was deserted. There was no sign of an apologetic driver returning. I banged the car roof with my fist in a fit of pique, tempted to finger a rude message across the dust. But one of the penalties of being a doctor in a medium-sized town was the terror of being seen doing something unworthy of your status. Headlines read so well, and local papers can be merciless to fallen angels. 'Doctor vandalises car' sounded a suitable headline, especially if they quoted some of my choice language. So I gave up, threw my passenger door wide open, flipped the top on the sharps box, pricking myself with a needle, moved the stuff off the seat and clambered clumsily across before reaching the driving seat. I'd also caught my skirt on the gear stick. Hot, sweaty and cross I eased the Carlton out of the parking lot, somehow managing to avoid scraping the Lada. Then I slipped the car into gear and moved off.

It was Rosie with her sharp, little-girl's eyes who drew my attention to the mark on the side of my door.

Someone had drawn a crude cartoon of a heart pierced by an arrow.

Chapter Seven

The print gave my dreams a vivid form. It haunted me. The child now always appeared with her arms clasped around the toadstool, before she moved towards the mound of red-brown earth and sat, stroking. And sometimes, in these dreams, she would hum as she climbed the rotting tree stump.

It was the Sunday following my lunch with Ruth. The weather had broken and turned dull and wet, cold even. The weather had seemed to keep everyone on the estate indoors. The day was quiet with few emergency visits and my pager was mercifully silent. After a typically unsettled day Rosie and I sat down in the evening to watch a video. At nine o'clock, yawning, she went to bed and I sat and fidgeted in the lounge, trying to read a book, one ear cocked for the sound of the bleep. After the undisturbed day I anticipated a quiet night. I was wrong.

At eleven, just when I was considering going to bed, my pager gave a feeble bleep and displayed a message:

84-year-old woman fallen out of bed.

There was a telephone number and an address which meant nothing to me.

I picked up the telephone and dialled the number unenthusiastically. 'Doctor Lamont here.'

'I think you should come and look at my mother, Amelia.' It was a soft, clinging voice, yet at the time I failed to recognise it.

'What seems to be the trouble?'

'She's fallen out of bed.' The soft voice paused. 'I presume you got the message.'

I bit my tongue against the inevitable reply. At eighty-four I knew the likelihood was that she had broken something.

'Can you see any obvious injury?'

There was a pause before a hesitant, 'No.'

'Is she in pain?'

Again there was a pause, shorter this time as though the person on the other end needed to consider his answer carefully.

Eventually it came. 'Yes. She has hurt herself. Not badly but she is undoubtedly hurt and shocked.'

It wasn't quite what I had asked. Nevertheless . . . 'Whereabouts?'

'In her leg. She's hurt her leg.' There was a deliberation in his manner that made me resentful. Or maybe it was that I knew I would have to turn out.

I had only one available cop-out. 'Who's her doctor?'

'You are, Harriet.'

Then I knew who it was. He had summoned me and I knew I must go as he had always meant me to. It was with an awful sense of fatalism that I asked my next question. 'Where do you live?'

'In the cottage at the end of Gordon's Lane.'

I knew Gordon's Lane. It was a narrow, little-used road to the south of the town following a left turn towards the forest and across the causeway over the Heron Pool. But instead of turning right, to Vera Carnforth's, you turn sharp left. 'I didn't know there was a cottage there.'

'There is,' the soft, polite voice answered, 'and that's where you'll find us. Me and my mother. Just turn left at the Heron Pool and climb the hill in the direction of the trees. I'll leave the outside light on to guide you.' He put the phone down.

I had no option but to go.

I peeped in on Rosie. She was asleep, arms flailing, her pale hair strewn across the pillow like ghostly seaweed. I closed the door gently without waking her. If you enjoy your sleep, my darling, don't be a doctor.

I hated leaving her. Every time I vowed would be the last. I would sort something out – somehow.

I knew it was a silly, superstitious thing to do even as I scribbled the note and left it by the phone? *'Eleven o five. I have been called out to see Mrs Pritchard, Gordon's Lane.'*

I propped it up against the phone as insurance even though I knew that the pager service would have logged the call. Then I pulled on a cardigan over my shirt and locked the door behind me, crunching over the gravel to the car. It seemed much later than eleven ten.

After such a dull day the clouds must have cleared. It was a beautiful night, one I might have wasted indoors had I not been forced to visit this woman. A star-spangled, navy canopied night, silent apart from a dog who was giving short, staccato barks from the other side of the estate. Maybe it was I who was disturbing him. No one else was around. For once there was no sound of traffic, no screaming police cars, no bustle, no people. The entire estate slept or was inside, enjoying the evening as I was not able to. I turned the engine on, tuned in to Classic FM, and pulled out of the drive to a haunting, Chopin nocturne, E minor. The headlights seemed obscenely bright as I swung out of the road and headed south.

I drove through the town to where the forest rose to the left and the Cheshire plain was a blank expanse on my right. Two miles along the main road I turned into the forest and passed the Heron Pool. Tonight it had been magicked into black glass which shattered my headlights into shards as the wind blew across the water and smashed the moon into yet more silvery shapes. It was so beautiful I could almost feel grateful to my patient for luring me out into the night instead of letting me shelter from it.

Had it not been that the summoning patient was Pritchard.

With a paralysing air of fatalism I crossed the causeway and turned left into the narrow lane where Rosie and I had wandered during the heatwave. Then I took a sharp right turn up Gordon's Lane. This was the remoter side of the forest, a confusing area where a myriad of tiny lanes formed a maze which could be tricky to navigate. It would be easy to get lost. On the radio the announcer confirmed the Chopin nocturne was E minor before switching to a tidy drawing room piano piece. I didn't recognise it and contemplated doing Theseus' trick with a ball of red string to make sure I found my way back home again. But it felt like a one-way journey.

I opened my car window to breathe in scented air and draw in the private shrieks of the night and then I heard another distant bark. But a fox this time. I was tingling alive now, my nerves raw, seeming to hear everything the night had to offer and I consoled myself. Maybe turning out at this time wasn't so bad after all and my mind shifted to wonder in what state I would find this old lady. I eyed my Gladstone bag on the passenger seat. I carried some analgesia in there. Nothing too strong. I didn't want to tempt Danny Small to raid my car. Just some Fortral, a syringe, a few needles. If she was bruised but not badly harmed a shot in the leg should relieve any pain. But if there was even a suspicion that something was broken I would simply send her into hospital. For a brief second my sympathy was not with the fallen geriatric but the poor sod of a houseman who would have to spend half an hour taking a history, organising X-Rays and drawing blood.

I picked up my A-Z, just to check the route although I knew where to go. The only thing I didn't know was where Pritchard's cottage was.

I bumped through the black void towards a faint gleam of light slightly to my left. The hedges were tall and untrimmed, high enough to form a tunnel through which my car passed, meeting gleams of moonlight when the branches thinned, but the faint light stood out like a yellow beacon at the end. This was a quiet spot. There must be no other houses along this lane and virtually no traffic. Grass grew up the centre, softly grazing the bottom of my car.

It wasn't so much a cottage as a corrugated tin shack and Pritchard was standing outside, watching for me. My car headlights picked out his portly shape but I couldn't see all of his face as his hand was shielding his eyes from the glare. I turned the engine and lights off, opened the door and stepped out.

'Hello, Mr Pritchard.'

He gave me one of his strange smiles. 'I'm so glad you came. My mother is very upset.'

I eyed the dimly lit shack. I didn't want to go in. 'Where is she?' I must do my job, treat the old lady and get back to Rosie. Mentally I added a please.

The night seemed too still and Pritchard was staring too intently. His mouth quivered. 'You seem on edge if I might say so.'

'It's eleven o clock,' I snapped. 'I'm anxious to get home to my daughter.'

He opened his mouth to say something. For one awful moment I thought he was going to put a hand on my shoulder but he changed his mind, backing into a dingy room filled with stale air and lumpy, brown utility furniture. I followed him. Above us a forty-watt bulb was swinging in a yellow shade shaped like a Chinese coolie hat. In the corner stood an ancient TV set and through a half-open door to the right I caught a glimpse of a kettle standing on a Belling cooker. I might have known Pritchard would live in such squalor.

He stood in the centre of the room making no move, studying me. 'It is nice to see you here,' he said, 'in my home. I've had visions of you coming here.'

'Mr Pritchard,' I said. My voice sounded hollow, thin, reedy and frightened. 'It's late. Let me see your . . .' But I was already aware that there was no sign or sound of any other person in the house. What if there was no mother? What if . . . I fixed on a door, ajar, on the left. A bedroom door? 'Where's the patient?'

He didn't move. Behind the owlish glasses he didn't even blink.

'The patient,' I repeated hoarsely.

He still stared at me. 'Before you see her,' he said, hesitating, 'I think I should explain something.' I waited rigidly, listening to the sound of my chest rising and falling.

'My mother.' He cleared his throat. 'My mother is a sick woman although she pretends she isn't.'

I bit back the retort that that was why I was here. I was a doctor, for goodness' sake. Let me see the patient and go.

He cleared his throat again. 'Sometimes she thinks. No,' he corrected himself, '*imagines* is the word. She imagines things.'

I was relieved there *was* a mother It made me brave. 'What do you mean, Mr Pritchard, imagines things?'

He took a short step towards me. 'She suffers,' he said with the air of a magician producing a rabbit from a hat, 'from delusions.'

'Is it a delusion then that she fell out of bed?' I stepped towards him. 'Is she deluded that she is hurt?'

'No, no nothing like that. Nothing.' He laughed through his nose. 'Other things.' He was keeping his secrets to himself.

'She did fall and she has hurt herself. But . . .' He pondered the point. 'Yes – indeed she has.'

'Then let me see her.' I spotted a door to the left. 'Is she in there?'

He gave another of his strange, patronising smiles. 'Oh yes,' he said. 'She doesn't go out except rarely.'

The bedroom was almost filled by a huge, high bed with bars at its top and bottom. A satin quilt had slipped to one side. She was at the far end of the room on the floor; a crumpled, groaning heap. And it was cold. I was wearing a cardigan and I was cold. A billowing curtain confirmed that the window was open. And from what I could see beneath another dingy light, the old woman was twisted on the floor; I could see white hair, frightened eyes, lips blue from the cold. But she was real, no figment of Pritchard's imagination.

I could guess what had happened. There was a commode just behind the door. She had obviously got muddled, thought it was the other side, had tried to climb out to use it, squatted, grabbed the counterpane and it had let her down, sliding to the floor with her. It had probably cushioned her fall and saved her from serious injury. But in ancient, osteoporotic old women like this even a soft fall could be enough to snap fragile bones. And she did seem in agony, her fingers knotting the quilt.

She was typical of her generation of war-survivors, iron grey hair in skinny plaits and a long flannelette nightie that gave out only the faintest odour of stale urine. Maybe she was unclean, but almost certainly not incontinent. I approached beneath another swinging forty-watt bulb dressed in a yellowed, Chinese coolie lampshade. They must have been selling them cheaply one day in the 1940s.

Amelia Pritchard wasn't exactly delighted to see me. Her sharp little eyes stared at me with hostility. 'Who are you?' Her voice was thin and reedy, cutting as a paper's edge.

I can be short too, especially halfway through the night. 'I'm the doctor,' I said, snapping the window shut. 'Let's have a look at you.' I pulled the quilt from her; lifted her nightie, felt her limbs. She groaned a little but there were no bones displaced and she had full movement in two arms and two legs. Added to that her conscious state was all it should be. She might be bruised and cold but there appeared to be nothing worse.

'Shall we get her back to bed?' I said to Pritchard.

Instantly he was behind me, breathing down my neck, polluting the air with his stale scent.

'I didn't like to move her,' he said, 'not until you'd checked her over. I might have done further damage.' He had a very slight speech impediment, a faint whistle through a gap between his two top incisors and the smell of stale sweat was even more overpowering than it had been in my surgery. I shifted away.

Pritchard and I manhandled the protesting old lady back into the high bed and I had a slightly better look at her, a quick palpation of her limbs. I could find nothing wrong. This time she'd been lucky. With relief I turned to leave but the old lady grabbed my arm with a maniac's iron grip. 'It was in the wrong place,' she said. 'Someone must have moved it.' She was looking at the corner of the room where she had fallen. I took little notice. I had met this before, many times: old lady, confused but always right. They're never wrong. It's everyone else who is mistaken.

Heaven help me. How often do we read more into grey hair than we should? Because she was old I assumed she was confused. Purely because she was old, I thought she was rambling.

'Now, mother.' Pritchard was fussing over her; tucking the quilt around her thin shoulders. There was calm sympathy in his voice with the vaguest hint of patronage. I ignored it. I wanted to escape.

And Amelia didn't seem that impressed with me. She was working her jaw to spit venom at her son. 'I told you not to get someone out.' Her voice was querulous and miserable. 'I warned you. What good's she done?'

Great, I thought, folding my stethoscope and snapping my bag shut. So appreciated. Feeling less than benevolent I returned the sour look. She might have been able to speak better if she had had her false teeth in.

She stuck her face close to mine and I could almost smell its meanness. 'We don't like people coming here.' Her venom was wasted on me. 'Why do you think we chose

91

to live in this spot in the first place?' She looked at neither of us as she muttered, 'Gossips.'

For the first time ever I felt some sympathy towards Pritchard Junior. He had his work cut out here. 'It's a good job he did call me, Mrs Pritchard,' I said crisply. 'Otherwise you would have frozen on the floor.'

She lowered her baggy eyelids and swallowed. She didn't like that, being grateful to him. The old lady was still shouting after me as I left the room. 'It was in the wrong place, you stupid girl,' she called out.

I wasn't listening.

As I left the bedroom I heard Pritchard's voice. 'Mother.' And I glanced back. This time his voice was even softer. Yet, paradoxically, the old lady looked even more cowed, with her head dropped on to her chest. I would have to call back in the morning.

Chapter Eight

I returned to a sleepy, confused Rosie and decided in future I must ask Sylvie to stay with her overnight when I was on call. So far I had been lucky. Nothing had happened, but Rosie was only nine years old. It wasn't even legal to leave her alone. And while she understood that occasionally I needed to go out to visit sick people in the middle of the night it didn't stop her from being frightened. Until this year Robin had almost always been around but now he wasn't and I could not afford to leave her with anyone else.

That was only one of my worries. For the rest of that night I could not sleep because every time I closed my eyes I could see the interior of that shabby cottage, smell Pritchard's scent and feel the fright of the old woman. As I had felt disturbed by the atmosphere there part, at least, of that atmosphere had been the old lady herself, querulous, intimidated. I could not forget her calling out to me even though she had disliked me, resented my presence and certainly had not trusted me. Yet she had tried to call me back. There had been a pathetic desperation in her voice. Something was wrong there and I had to go back. Night visits were risky. No matter how much common sense told me Pritchard was not a threat it didn't help me get over my revulsion for him, because instinct was telling me something else. He was an unsavoury character and he wanted to be close to me. On a warm night I was shivering.

I was showered and dressed a full hour before it was time to wake Rosie and in the dull light of a rainy morning I could almost convince myself that I had dreamed the whole thing. *Almost* convince myself. And then I drove Rosie to school.

A dark blue Lada is not such an uncommon car, is it? Surely it must be coincidence that I watched Rosie skip past one in the school car park?

The thought occupied my mind until I pulled up outside the surgery and met Neil in the car park.

He waited for me to lock my car. 'Good morning, Harry. Busy night last night?'

The bond between us was strengthening. After all, we had common ground. We were both discarded partners, in a way. The age gap wasn't enormous and we worked together, so we had fallen into the habit of giving each other lifts to the local medical meetings and once or twice he had come round in the evening to play draughts with Rosie, while I cooked. I felt much more comfortable in Neil's presence than Duncan's, for while Duncan studiously avoided all mention of Robin, Neil had the ability to throw his name, quite casually, into the conversation without it causing me hurt. It all helped.

'I got called out at eleven.'

He looked unsympathetic.

'But I couldn't sleep afterwards.'

'That's the trouble sometimes. Mind races, doesn't it?' He gave one of his straight-lipped smiles. 'I sometimes think my mind only starts working after I've left the patient's house. At the time all I'm really thinking of is getting back home again to a nice, warm bed.'

'Neil,' I began tentatively.

'Mm?'

'Have you ever felt . . . uncomfortable in someone's house?'

'Frequently.'

'I – I mean really uncomfortable. Frightened?'

Neil looked serious. 'Once or twice,' he said. 'Druggies mainly.'

'What about . . .'

He interrupted. 'And the odd schizophrenic who's been discharged into the community straight from a locked

94

ward. That happened once. He had a knife. I was pretty scared then.' He gave me a hard stare. 'Why? Something like that happen to you last night?'

I shook my head. It had been nothing to compare with either of those experiences. It had been a *feeling*. No more.

Neil seemed more interested in the medical aspect. Anything complicated?'

'No,' I said. 'Only an old lady who fell out of bed.'

He shrugged. We both knew it happened all the time. 'Send her into hospital?'

'No.' I paused. 'It wasn't necessary. She was OK. A bit grumpy and eccentric. Confused, maybe, but there was no indication to send her in. Nothing broken. Besides – her son was more than willing to look after her. Damned lucky really when offspring turn nursemaid.'

A spasm crossed his face and I cursed myself. I had not meant to hurt his feelings. To cover my embarrassment I gabbled a bit more than I had meant to about the visit.

'It was a dump of a place.'

'Plenty of those around. On the Dune's Estate?'

'No, along Gordon's Lane.'

But I could tell he was still abstracted by my comment and I cursed myself again. How could I have been so insensitive when the silence from his son must be so painful?

Neil was giving me such a strange look that for one dreadful minute I believed he was reading my mind. Instead he said, 'I didn't know there was a house along Gordon's Road. I thought it was a dead end.'

And it brought me back to the present. 'If you can call it a house,' I said. 'It's a tin shack, not much bigger than a chicken coop.' I made a face. 'Not much cleaner either.' Memories of the fusty atmosphere returned to nauseate me.

Neil was perceptive. 'I can see it made quite an impression on you.'

'Unfavourable,' I said, and recalled his lack of sympathy when I had complained about Anthony Pritchard. I decided to close the subject.

The trouble was Neil seemed to want to pursue the matter. 'I can't recall ever visiting anyone there. You do mean turn left after the pool?'

'The Heron Pool.' That vague vision of the child clasping the toadstool flicked in front of my eyes.

And the name seemed to mean something to Neil too. A spasm crossed his face. 'Is that what you call it?'

'There's a sign there,' I said. 'Heronry.'

'Mmm.' There was an awful, haunting sadness about his face. He was struggling to keep the conversation light and rational. 'And you say they're patients of ours?'

'That's right.'

'Been on the list long?' His laugh was almost back to normal. 'They must be an undemanding family.'

'Years,' I said. 'Don't you remember that creep Pritchard who kept coming to see me about his blood pressure?'

'The one with the dubious family history?' It was Neil's pleasure to mock me.

But I could laugh too. Oh yes. In the light of day and the comfort of the surgery, tales of poisoned fathers, unease at a sordid home visit, a patient who was overfamiliar with my Christian name and pestered to have his blood pressure taken. All these things could seem funny.

'It was his mother I saw and she's a bad tempered old biddy.' My detachment was growing by the minute. Even the memory of the old woman, waving stick-arms into the air, failed to disturb me. 'And no less peculiar than the son.'

Neil laughed and turned his key in the door 'Well,' he said. 'I still don't recall her even from your description.'

'I thought I'd go back today and take a better look at her. She is in her eighties and it was so dim there last night I couldn't examine her properly.'

Maybe Neil did sense my unease. Or perhaps he had another motive, but he offered to go for me anyway.

I appreciated the gesture but knew it had to be me who returned. 'No, no. It's OK. Really. Don't worry. I just need to pop in. I should check her out a bit more thoroughly. With a bit of luck Weirdo Pritchard won't even be there.'

'Well.' He hesitated, his box of notes under his arm. 'If you want anything . . .'

Patients' notes were filed in the reception area, in brown folders known as Lloyd George envelopes. The promise of care from cradle to grave was never more ably displayed than here, where National Health milk records, ancient letters describing outdated treatments, inoculations and examinations were all here for professional eyes to read. Clues to a person's entire life were contained in these envelopes.

I was curious about Mr Pritchard, Senior. I found the letter P on the rack then took out the two, thin folders that belonged to the sole inhabitants of Gordon's Lane. I had already read Anthony's recent notes and there was little to add from his childhood besides club feet when he was a toddler. And judging by the letter from the orthopaedic surgeon the treatment had been braces. Two-year-old Anthony Pritchard had, it seemed, screamed for the entire period of wearing them.

Now for his mother. I shook Amelia's notes out onto the desk. She had been born in the year the First World War had broken out, surely an ill omen to begin with. But her medical notes only extended as far back as the 1930s when she had joined the Silkworkers' Union so had bought health cover years before the National Health Service had taken over. In 1934 she had married and after ten years young Anthony arrived on the scene when his mother was thirty years old. He was born during the Second World War, in 1944, a year or two before the birth rate had bulged. Maybe his father had not been in the forces. Or maybe he had been granted leave to visit his wife. Who knows? The child had been conceived and as the National Health Service had been born Amelia Pritchard had visited her doctor frequently, on average once a month.

The doctor's writing was dreadful. I could hardly read some of the early entries except to make out odd injuries, fractures. The sign was the same now as it had always been: #. Ribs, a wrist, plus bruises and black eyes . . . It was a familiar picture of marital violence. And the young Anthony must have witnessed everything. He hadn't had a good start. Until he was six.

In 1950 the injuries had stopped abruptly. Husband died. I stared at the next word, clearly written in capitals and red ink. POISON. Underneath the doctor had scrawled two words. I took the first one to be a woman's name, *Anita*. The *A* was quite plain, the rest of the word illegible but certainly contained a crossed *T*. The second word began with a V. Beyond that I could not read. I imagined it was a woman's name and wondered whether Pritchard Senior had had a mistress. Underneath that the doctor had pencilled in, *I wonder.*

I did too. Doctors in the 1940s had never thought anyone except other doctors would ever read their notes. Hence they had ventured dangerous, sometimes libellous opinions. What a long time ago it had all been. Pritchard was dead and forgotten. Until I had asked his son about his cause of death.

And what did it have to do with the present? Probably nothing except that I knew that her husband's death had brought Amelia Pritchard a pleasanter, safer life. But like the doctor whose words and signature I could not read, I wondered.

The coroner's verdict, plainly copied out in red ink and capital letters, was unequivocal, Accidental Death. Perhaps, I reasoned, as well as being an accidental death it had been a convenient death.

So the steps of the jig became more complicated.

I spent the rest of the morning ploughing through a very average surgery with no worse pathology than a nasty case of bronchitis before leaving at eleven. The picture from the antique shop had stayed at the back of my mind. I wanted to take another look at it, maybe even buy it. To myself I could admit that to hang it in the house would be a dangerous move. It would be like giving in, like letting the events invade my own home. But they were already implanted, I argued. What would be the difference? I didn't know but some vague instinct told me this. That for the child to assume a more tangible form, even if it was through the medium of a rather cheap, 1920s print, would remove some of the mystical quality of the story that had no ending.

As I drove through the narrow streets of the town I found myself pondering another angle. Maybe absorbing the picture I would be able to convince myself that the child had not been murdered but had vanished somewhere, protected by the magic of a poisonous toadstool. And then maybe the dreams would stop because there had been something about the innocence of the child clinging to the thick stalk that reminded me too much of Rosie. She had the same hurt, clear stare.

Old habits die hard. I parked in the same car park as before, but this time safely between a Renault caravanette and a pink Mini. I wouldn't be long. Then again I climbed the narrow street towards the antiques shop, thoughts still fixed on Melanie Carnforth. Something must have happened to her. She couldn't really have vanished. There had to be an answer. But in a 1920s print?

An electronic buzzer sounded like an angry wasp as I stepped inside the shop. It wasn't the best quality of places. The clocks were all Edwardian, the pictures prints rather than originals and the only decent piece of furniture was a reproduction mahogany desk. There was no sign of the picnic basket, it must have been sold. But the shop wasn't empty of customers. There was a couple at the counter, well dressed, in his 'n' hers dark business suits. They were choosing some silver serviette rings. I listened to their prattle, glancing around the walls of the shop to look for the print. I couldn't see it.

I studied the walls, peered around the smaller back room. I still couldn't see it. There was another room upstairs but here the walls were bare apart from a wall clock with an irregular tick like a damaged heart and a dreadful modern oil, splashes of oranges and blues. There was no title, I noticed, and it was unsigned. I wasn't surprised.

When I returned to the front counter the couple were still deliberating over the silver serviette rings and I began to get fidgety. Apart from Gordon's Lane I had two other calls in the council estate. And I wanted to get home to Rosie. I had promised to take her and one of the few faithful old friends to the pictures this afternoon to see the new Steven Spielberg before visiting a pizza parlour. I didn't want to let them down and I wasn't sure how long I would be at Gordon's Lane. At the same time I was painfully aware that the old guilt was surfacing again – almost her entire summer holidays were being spent farmed out with various friends. I had yet to ask Sylvie how she felt about spending the nights with Rosie on my nights on call. Maybe a foreign au pair was the answer. But for one child who was invariably at school?

'Excuse me.' At last the shop keeper apologised to the frisky couple and turned her attention to me. 'Can I help you?' They were the traditional words, but rudely spoken. She must already have assessed me as a mean spender. I was horribly aware of the loose denim dress, years old, even more years out of fashion compared with her dress which had all the fancy trimmings of expensive, designer stuff.

'You had a print.' I said. 'Nineteen-twenties I would imagine.'

'Yes?' I didn't know whether the yes was a yes of comprehension or confirmation but she was looking blank so I enlarged. 'It was of a child clasping a toad-stool.'

Her thickly lipsticked mouth gave a patronising smile as she fingered a label on the top pocket of her silk shirt-waister 'Lovely, wasn't it,' she cooed.

'I'd like to- ' I got no further.

'I'm afraid,' she said, 'it's sold.'

'Sold?'

'Funny how things go,' she said. 'We've had it for ages and then two people want to buy it.'

Now I felt cheated. 'Who bought it?'

My abruptness won her respect. 'A woman,' she said nicely. 'She came in yesterday morning and seemed to fall in love with it.'

Maybe it was that phrase that made my senses tingle, *fall in love with it.*

It alerted me. 'What did she look like?'

Now she was curious, very curious. 'Quite well dressed,' she said. 'But I can't tell you her name. She paid cash. It was only thirty pounds,' she said. 'It was just a print.' Now she was wondering what all the fuss was about. Had she sold something and missed its value? 'Was there something particular about the print?'

I hesitated. The three of them were watching me, the antique-shop owner and the couple. I felt foolish. 'Not really,' I said. 'I just liked it.' Then the lie. 'I thought it might look nice in my daughter's bedroom.'

The assistant, sensing a chance of a sale, swiftly consoled me. They often had prints of that era. They were never expensive. Some were even nicer than . . . Could she take my telephone number?

It was all efficient sales talk but I didn't want another print. I had wanted that one and someone had bought it first. 'It's OK,' I said. 'Thanks. I'll pop in again.'

Maybe it was my imagination or my lying, guilty conscience. But I felt all their eyes on me as I tramped back to my car. I knew it was significant that the print had been bought.

All the way back down to the car park I could visualise the picture in much more detail than I had thought I would have remembered. I had only viewed it at the back of the shop through a sunlit window. And yet I could picture every detail, the child's face, pressed hard against the stem. Not smiling. Pleased but not smiling. Her eyes looked knowing, as though she was aware that this beautiful object was death. And yet she was not frightened. Her hands were chubby, clasped around the stem, her cheek pressed so hard it had been pushed forward to seem fatter than it was. The red and white cap had formed a spotted canopy over her so her face was shaded. And at her feet were flowers, daisies, buttercups, cowslips. Meadow flowers, like the ones Melanie would have trodden through as she walked towards her boundary. Flowers like the ones Rosie and I had picked as we had sauntered along Gordon's Lane.

I reached my car still saturated with thoughts. Ruth was right. Melanie could not have fallen or she would have been found. Dead children don't bury their own bodies. They are found in tragic circumstances, at the bottom of a drop, or a well, fallen out of a tree, face down in a deep pond. Images came to me of deep, stagnant waters like the ones of the Heron Pool.

She could not be there. She would have been found. Surely one of the first things they would have done would have been to have dragged those dark waters or sent divers down.

Then where? Kidnap seemed a more likely alternative but in real life these things do not happen. Children are found, ransoms paid. Sometimes bodies are not. I wondered whether Vera had come to this conclusion or whether she continued to hope.

But if no one had been charged with the crime whoever had murdered Melanie was still free, somewhere, waiting.

I did my two town calls quickly before heading south towards the forest and was soon crossing the causeway over the Heron Pool. The blaze of sudden sunshine was blindingly reflected in the stagnant water and on the edge, almost hidden in the reeds, I saw the long neck of nature's best fisherman, a grey heron. Even as I watched he stabbed the water. When he straightened he was holding a wriggling fish in his beak. I took the left turn quickly followed by a sharp right.

Gordon's Lane looked different by daylight. The tall hedges were pretty. The verges splashed with wild flowers were just beginning to spot the green with colour; dandelions and daisies and tall cow parsley. A child would have loved to gather armfuls. They were a tempting sight.

As I approached the tin hut I realised it was not just the lane that looked different but the cottage too, rusting green, blending in with its background of trees and fields. This morning it wore its neglect quaintly. It reminded me of the gingerbread house of Hans Christian Andersen. But the gingerbread house had been inhabited by a witch. I pulled up in the concrete yard and noticed rampant climbers almost concealing the window panes. The place looked deserted.

I stepped out of the car. Damp days had left mud scars in the yard. And they supported an eco system of their own, grass and Welsh Poppies, dandelions, nettles and docks. I locked my car and then wondered why I had done so. There was no one around to steal it. Maybe it was an automatic reaction to unease. Lock, Protect, Safeguard what is yours.

As I approached the front door I realised what a secret, private place this was. The hedges had been left to reach their tallest state, making the entire approach a gloomy tunnel. The field beyond looked muddy and undrained.

Too mushy for cattle. The trees made it dark. Neil had been right – Gordon's Lane was a dead end. I could see a five-barred gate and beyond that a mud track that vanished into the trees.

I knocked on the door and wondered if the house was empty. Surely not. The old lady was in no fit state to go anywhere. And I had said I would visit today. I knocked again and opened the door. The sitting room was empty. Calling I went straight to the bedroom.

She shrieked when she saw me and tried to pull the covers over her face.

'It's all right,' I said. 'I'm the doctor. I came last night. Remember?'

She gave a reluctant shrug.

'I could do with examining you properly,' I said in a falsely hearty tone. 'It was late last night. I was a bit tired to do a thorough examination. Besides,' I tried to make a joke out of it, 'it's quite dark in here. They do make electric bulbs brighter than forty watt.' I took a step forward. 'I need to be sure that you're not hurt, Mrs Pritchard. Is that all right?'

She was more concerned with the mention of the light bulbs than the physical examination. 'Anthony doesn't like me to waste electricity,' she snapped.

I drew back the threadbare curtains. 'Well I can see OK today, anyway.'

For a brief moment her face was so hostile I thought she would refuse to co-operate with me. She would have been within her rights. But her stare softened. 'I don't suppose it'll do any harm.'

'I could do with your nightie off,' I said. 'I'll help you.'

I slipped it over her head. Skinny breasts, thin arms. Thin arms covered in bruises, all colours. Yellow, black, green blue. Old bruises, more recent bruises. 'Grabbers,' we call them. Bruises on the upper arm, as any child abuse specialist will tell you, are an indication of an arm that has

104

been held too firmly. Grabbers. Like father like son. It isn't only children who can be abused.

I could have ignored the bruises. Instead I decided to draw attention to them. 'Your son?' I said, touching the marks.

She didn't even look frightened. She simply met my curiosity with calm acceptance tinged with puzzlement that I should take so much notice.

Her pale eyes stared at me as I gave a cursory examination to the rest of her body. Apart from a nasty bruise on her left breast there was no more damage. Rough handling but no more. It was as I bent her forward to listen to her chest and examine her ribs and spine that the real clue came.

I was sitting on the bed behind her, my stethoscope placed over the base of her right lung. She was staring at the corner where I had found her last night.

I was learning now not to confront Amelia Pritchard full on. Instead I pretended to be percussing her spine. Surreptitiously I was following her gaze.

On the floor, in the corner, deeply indented in the carpet, were four small evenly spaced marks. It took me a minute or two to work out what they were and Amelia was getting impatient.

'Haven't you finished yet, doctor?' she snapped. 'I'm getting cold.'

I slipped the nightie back down over the iron grey hair and glanced in the opposite corner. I knew what had made those marks. The commode must have stood there for a long time to have made them so deep. He had moved it. He had wanted her to fall. He had wanted me to come out here.

Chapter Nine

So I had gained a new image to disturb me. By the end of June the vulnerable old woman in the forest had joined Melanie Carnforth to haunt my dreams. But unlike Melanie, Amelia Pritchard was a real, flesh and blood person, one who, as my patient, had the right to summon me, any time. When my pager gave its insistent bleep I dreaded reading her name.

It had occurred to me that Pritchard could make up any story at any time of the day or night to force me to visit his mother and I would have no excuse not to go. In a way it was worse that nothing had actually happened on the two occasions when I had been there. It meant that neither the police nor my partners would have any sympathy if I refused to attend. Neither would the Medical Defence Union back me up in the event of a complaint. So, perhaps stupidly, I kept my fears to myself and confided in no one. Like a coward I asked the Health Visitor to look in on Amelia Pritchard.

I thought that would be enough to protect her.

So I clung to my one consolation – Danny Small kept away from the surgery for the entire month of June and I was not defending my decision to refuse him methadone once or twice a week.

Pritchard stayed silent. But in July he came back again ostensibly to have his blood pressure checked. He didn't even mention his mother but while I pumped the sphyg-momanometer cuff up I caught him watching me.

'Your blood pressure's doing fine, Mr Pritchard.' I unhooked the earpieces from my ears, laid the stethoscope across the desk, folded the cuff away.

He said nothing but tugged his sleeve down. Summer and winter, Pritchard always wore the same clothes, a sweaty shirt, a moth-nibbled tie, a grubby jacket. In the months that I had been seeing him he had never varied this basic recipe. But however varied his colour schemes were they all looked as though they had been bought from charity shops. All were outdated fashions, well worn, overwashed, discarded. That morning he waited until he had fumbled his arms back into his jacket before saying what must have been on the tip of his tongue from the moment he had inched his way around the door. 'I do a good job you know,' he said, 'looking after my mother. I do have a day job as well.'

It did not cross my mind to ask him what his day job was. I imagined he would work at the back of a poky office, pen pushing, a danger to no one.

'I don't know why you can't acknowledge the fact that many sons would not take the care of their mother that I do.'

So he expected a pat on the back?

'There isn't any need for you to be sending the nurse in.' He paused to take breath. 'To check up on me. It isn't necessary.'

So that was what he wanted, a free hand to taunt the old lady. So why consult me at all? I watched him steadily.

'Why do you keep sending that nurse round all the time? We don't need her.'

'Your mother is a frail old woman,' I began.

'But nurses don't visit all the old ladies,' he said. 'Only my mother.'

'She had a fall.'

He glared at me. 'It was just the once,' he said. 'It was an accident. She wasn't badly hurt.' His pebble-lensed glasses fixed on me. His eyes were huge, distorted. 'You were the one who examined her, Harriet. If she had been badly hurt surely you would have noticed?'

I stiffened.

He put his face right up close to mine. 'She won't fall again. So call off your nurse. I'll mind my mother. And I'll see you next month.'

I knew I had to talk to someone or I would explode. I waylaid Neil in the car park the next morning.

'So what are you saying, Harriet? That he's ill treating the old lady?' He actually laughed, his teeth startling white against a deep tan. 'Granny bashing?'

'Yes, I think he . . .'

'She wasn't complaining, was she?'

I shook my head.

He gave me a sharp look. 'You're sure this isn't a case where your personal prejudices are coming to the fore?'

'What do you mean?'

'Well, Pritchard Junior does give you the creeps, doesn't he?'

'Yes, but-'

'And I agree he sounds a strange character.'

I realised that neither Neil nor Duncan had ever met Anthony Pritchard – nor his mother. It was I who Pritchard had homed in on. 'It's more than that.'

'Is he coming in to see you again?'

'He will,' I said grimly. 'He's decided his blood pressure needs monthly checks.'

'Then why don't you warn him off?'

'You mean . . .'

'Nothing too heavy. Just tell him you'll probably be checking up on his mother frequently and that part of that check is a physical examination.'

'But it isn't,' I objected.

'Pritchard won't know that, will he?' Neil thought for a moment. 'You could get the Social Services involved but I really wouldn't advise it.' He scanned me thoughtfully as though assessing how amenable I was to his suggestions. 'Look at it this way. There isn't much to go on, is there? Old ladies bruise easily. And if you say she's making no complaint and the Health Visitor hasn't found anything wrong?'

'I know he moved the commode. I saw the marks.' Even I hesitated to tell Neil that I had deduced that the commode had been moved purely to draw me out to the hut. So of course Neil viewed the incident from the other angle. 'A very weak assault, Harry. Oh come on. And besides, now he knows you are alert, the old lady will probably be safe.'

It was then that I began to realise how very clever Neil was. Almost in a legal fashion he had put the entire problem into perspective. Worse, I had to acknowledge that his was the voice of reason and I felt wrong footed for having unburdened my problem on to him – on his very first day back from his trip to Turkey. I tried to rectify matters self-consciously. 'Was your holiday good?'

'Excellent,' he said enthusiastically. 'Absolutely marvellous. I haven't had such a good time in ages.'

'Where was it you went?'

'Istanbul.' His eyes lit up. 'What a place. The mosques, and the amazing sights.' He grinned. 'I even went to a belly dancer's night club.'

'Oh.' For some silly reason this confession embarrassed me. I had never thought of Neil in a sexual context. He was, simply, Neil. Friend, colleague, doctor.

It was just one of my many mistakes in that year.

To cover my confusion I added, 'Lots of photos, I expect.'

'Absolutely. Lots. Not in the album yet though. And tell me. How's my best girl?'

'Rosie's missed you,' I said. 'She says I don't play draughts with half as much . . . what was the word she used? Oh I know. Strategy.' I tapped his shoulder playfully. 'Now I wouldn't have called draughts a game of strategy at all.'

He burst out laughing. 'You have to keep the youngsters occupied.'

'Well you seem to have done that,' I said. 'Look, why don't you come round tomorrow? We'll have a takeaway curry.'

His eyes lit up. Maybe after the holiday returning to isolation seemed doubly lonely. For a fleeting moment I was angry with Petra – and with Sandy too. They should not have left him alone. He deserved better than this.

My first patient of the morning was Ruth, bearing a urine sample in a little plastic bottle which she triumphantly placed on my desk. 'I'm sure it's positive,' she said. 'Absolutely sure. I've missed a period. And my breasts feel like lead weights. Harry,' she said delightedly, 'I even feel sick in the mornings.'

'And luckily for you,' I said, 'I have a home pregnancy kit.' I eyed the miniature Bells whisky bottle. 'It is an early morning specimen, isn't it?'

She nodded and watched me fish the testing kit out of the drawer. 'You know I feel Arthur should be here,' she said, hands clasped together. 'I'm so excited.'

I opened the bottle, filled the dropper and put the requisite number of drops of urine on the reagent strip. Then it was just a matter of waiting. Only for a few seconds, less than a minute, but Ruth's exuberance was infecting me. I badly wanted her to be pregnant. But I also wanted the baby to be normal. A swift glance at her face told me how very much this all meant to her. I found it almost threatening.

The line turned blue and Ruth stared at me. 'It's positive,' she whispered. 'I am pregnant.' And her hands crept over her stomach as though she was feeling for the baby.

I laughed uneasily. 'It's nowhere near there yet, Ruth. It's not even peeping over your symphysis pubis. Congratulations,' I said heartily. 'I don't quite know how you've done it so quickly but you really are pregnant. These tests are very accurate.' I glanced at my gestation disc. 'By my calculations you should have an April baby, Ruth.' But even then I felt obliged to add, 'You know . .... .'

'Don't spoil my fun, Harry,' she warned. 'I know I'll need tests and scans and more tests and more scans. And still, because of my age no one will believe me capable of

110

bearing a normal child.' There was a tinge of bitterness in both her words and her face. 'And every time any one of those tests is done I'll worry that they'll find something and some nice professional like you will only do your job and persuade me . . .' She put her hand on my arm, 'oh ever so nicely, what the sensible thing to do is. But for now just let me enjoy it, please. Back off and let me be happy.'

Medicine never allowed me to be one hundred per cent happy. And that made me let Ruth down. Instead of pure joy I had tempered it too much with caution. I was thoughtful throughout the entire morning.

I was still thoughtful when Duncan walked in. I watched him carefully as he poured his coffee from the pot, and asked after his wife. 'Duncan,' I said, 'How's Fiona these days?'

He drew in a long, deep breath. 'Not good,' he said.

'What's the matter?'

He leaned back in his chair. 'She's very lonely, missing Merryn,' he said finally.

Merryn was their daughter. 'She isn't at home any more?'

'The nearest decent job she can get is Manchester. It's fifty miles away. And with the on-call commitment she finds it difficult to get over and see us.'

'I'll pop up and see Fiona,' I promised.

His face lit up. 'Oh, that would be good. She's fond of you.' He paused. 'No, wait. I've got a better idea. Harriet,' he said. 'It's our wedding anniversary next week. Merryn's promised to come over and cook us a meal. Why not come then?'

'What night? I'm on call . . .'

'Wednesday.'

'Hadn't you better check with . . .?'

'No,' he said. 'I know it will be all right. Please, come over on Wednesday.'

The gesture both pleased and touched me. I really was fond of Duncan, Fiona and Merryn. She too was a doctor, at the moment training to be a GP.

Neil raised his eyebrows when I asked him to babysit.

We were in my lounge, sprawled across the sofa. The takeaway curry had been eaten, the debris cleared straight into the dustbin, Rosie had won at draughts and been tucked up in bed and now we were finishing off the bottle of wine. In the background a classic CD was playing almost too quietly to hear. A lamp burned in the corner.

'So,' Neil said, 'Duncan's decided to make peace with you.'

'We were never at war.'

'I think,' he said smiling, 'that Duncan took it as a sign of rampant feminism the way you threw Robin out.'

'That's nonsense' I said uneasily. 'It wasn't like that at all.'

'Tales abound,' he was still smiling, 'of a suitcase bursting open as it fell from a first-floor window?'

Now I laughed too. 'It seemed quicker than lugging it down the stairs,' I said. 'You know how Robin always loved clothes. It was heavy. What are you laughing at?'

'You,' he said. 'Do you know you're changing?'

'In what way?'

'Less vulnerable,' he said. 'More detached, stronger. And I think you've been buying yourself some new clothes.'

Now I felt decidedly coy. 'Maybe just a couple.'

'Well I approve,' he said. 'And I'll certainly Rosie-sit again next Wednesday, even if the cat does snag my trousers.'

It was only as he left that I wondered, why *had Duncan asked me to dinner but not Neil?* Our practice was not on call tonight. A neighbouring doctor was covering under a reciprocal agreement. As we covered their patients too. As far as I knew there was no animosity between my two colleagues. *So why just me?*

Was it because Duncan wanted to discourage our growing friendship? Surely not. Surely he could not still hold out any hope that Robin and I would fall into each other's arms again.

Unless he knew something I didn't. About Janina? About Robin? Or did he want to discourage our growing friendship because he knew something about Neil?

Duncan lived to the north of Larkdale, on a hillside bordered by the same forest which skirted round the back of the ridge and overlooked the town, finally ending a couple of miles beyond Gordon's Lane and the Carnforths' smallholding. His house was reached by a rough, stony track but there were only four houses along it, the last one a farm. None of the inhabitants had been prepared to go to the expense of having the road tarmacked, so I bumped and lurched the half mile from the road and fretted about my silencer.

I don't know when I became aware that someone was following me. Even on a summer's evening and a lonely road it can be difficult to know what is coincidence and what is not. The blue Lada may just have happened to be going the same way. I didn't really notice it until I turned up the rough track.

It was close behind me, crowding me. It had to be going to one of the four houses. There was no public right of way. It looked large in my rear view mirror. I concentrated on staring forwards. The rocks in the centre could have been hazardous. I only let my eyes linger on the driver as I turned into Duncan's drive. It was Pritchard and he made no attempt either to speak, to wave or to acknowledge my presence. He simply stopped at the entrance.

I got out of my car, deliberately glanced in his direction, locked up and banged on Duncan's door.

Fiona opened it and gave me a warm hug. 'I'm so glad Duncan invited you, finally,' she said. 'I can't believe it was New Year's Eve when we last met.' I handed her the flowers and wished her a happy wedding anniversary before following her along their hall, remembering the first time I had come here, a shy junior partner with husband and baby in tow. Then I had wondered how Duncan, Fiona and Merryn had coped with such isolation. I found it threatening. It was only later, when I knew them all a little better, that I realised they thrived on being a self sealed unit, a family who neither wanted nor desired intrusion.

A dinner invite was a rare honour.

'I suppose New Year's Eve was the beginning of the end.' It was typical Fiona bluntness. I nodded. How perceptively she must have watched the three of us that night, myself, Robin and Janina, and seen quite clearly the way the wind would blow us all. 'I think life will be easier for you now, Harriet.' Having cleared the air deftly she added, 'What a lovely dress. Black does suit you, if it's in the right material. Nothing too slinky or sparkly.' Fiona was the only one who always called me Harriet and never Harry.

Except Pritchard. Why had he followed me tonight?

Duncan appeared in the doorway and distracted my thoughts. 'Harry,' he said warmly. 'I thought I heard your car.' We eyed each other cautiously and did not hug but gave each other a prolonged and friendly handshake.

At surgery Duncan was not a smart dresser but he passed the respectability test. At home he could have passed for a visiting hobo. His hair stuck out like wisps of straw, he wore a shapeless sweater in undyed sheep's wool with loops dangling where he had caught it, baggy cords, bald at the knees, and slippers bulging with toes. But he did look comfortable and content and as I followed them along the hall I could sense the warmth of this family home. I knew that our house in Larch Road had never held this atmosphere.

I handed Duncan the champagne and he made a pretence of studying the label.

'Australian. Very avant-garde of you, Harry. I'm sure Robin would have plumped for French stuff.'

It seemed a sign of approval that I had been accepted without Robin. So I settled comfortably into the sofa, sipped the dilute gin and tonic and asked Duncan how many years they'd been married.

'Twenty-eight,' he said, with real pride.

'Harriet.' Merryn was plumper than when I had last seen her but she was still as radiant as ever. She was one of those people who fills a room with their presence, with a wide smile, deep blue eyes and a loud, commanding voice which she had a habit of modulating at intervals. It had the effect of making you listen. 'How are you?'

She was not a beautiful woman. Not even those who loved her would claim she was. But those who loved her numbered almost every single person who had met her. She radiated warmth, inspired trust and showed an optimistic conviction that everyone would live up to her high ideals. Some sour little part of me might have resented her. She was certainly a better doctor than I and the reason for that had nothing to do with clinical acumen. In that I honestly believed we were equal. The reason was that Merryn loved people while I did not. I treated people. Sometimes I cured people. Sometimes not. But it was not through love for the human race that I was a doctor. I knew that underneath I did not love its 'silly face' as she did. To Merryn medicine was a vocation. To me a job.

She bent and kissed both my cheeks, but it was not the affected air kiss of the chattering classes.

'Well you look brilliant.' She turned. 'Doesn't she, Mum?'

'Most definitely.'

Merryn's face visibly relaxed as though she had suffered my marital break up alongside me. And that was the trouble. She probably had.

'Bloody Robin,' she said, draining the small, square-cut glass which I knew would contain neat whisky. 'Didn't know when he was well off. I mean *that bimbo.*'

It was exactly what I wanted to hear.

Merryn poured herself another whisky, peered at my almost full glass and topped up both her mother's and her father's glasses.

'Mind you, Harry,' she said. 'I don't know how you put up with him. He was a dreadful philanderer.'

'Merryn.' Fiona was protesting weakly.

'Well he was, Mum.' She looked back at me. 'I suppose the trouble was he was so good looking women made a bit of a play for him.'

I diverted the talk to her job hunt. Her three years GP training were up soon and she needed a practice of her own.

'It's hopeless,' she said gloomily. 'There isn't a thing within fifty miles of here. There just aren't the jobs. At least not in the decent practices. After all, this is largely a rural area and the partnerships are, by and large, stable.'

A swift glance passed between father and daughter.

Duncan made it a touch too clear that if a vacancy was to occur in our practice she would be his first choice. It didn't take a huge imagination to fill in the gaps. If I resigned Merryn would fill my place without Duncan feeling even a tinge of regret. And to Fiona, to have her daughter home again would be heaven.

'Come on,' Merryn said abruptly, flipping her whisky glass back down on the wine table, making it rock. 'Let's eat. I'm starving.'

We followed her into the dining room. It looked celebratory, almost bridal, with a stunning white tablecloth, silver candles flickering in tall, branched candlesticks. There was a scent of beeswax and although it was July and a warm night, logs flickered in the grate.

I didn't notice it at first. The Fairleys had taste, a few choice pieces of silver, a lovely oil over the fireplace, a mahogany card table in the alcove at the far end of the room on which stood a lamp with a pale green lampshade. No Chinese coolie hat here. Fiona Fairley was a talented homemaker and she and Duncan regularly scoured local antique shops and fairs for choice items. He would often describe some 'bargain' he had picked up for a song. Tonight the silver had been cleaned; the plates reflected the firelight so well they looked as though they had been polished. The green rocket salad, fresh smoked Scottish salmon and slices of lemon could have been served up in the best restaurant in the country and from the kitchen wafted an appetising scent. Venison, I guessed. It smelt strong.

Duncan poured us each a small glass of champagne and raised a toast. 'To partnerships, Harry,' he said. 'Health, happiness, good fortune and legal medicine.' His eyes were sparkling. 'And maybe even a smidgin of romance.'

'You can spare me that,' I said.

It was then that I glanced into the alcove over the beam of the lamp. The glow picked out the print of the child clasping a toadstool. I stared and stared at it until Fiona spoke.

'You like it?'

'Yes,' I said quietly. 'I do like it.'

'We bought it-'

'I know where you bought it,' I said. 'I saw it in the shop. I was thinking of buying it myself. But it was closed. And then-'

'We bought it as a wedding anniversary present, to each other.'

'What a coincidence. Both of you going for the same print,' Merryn said brightly. 'And yet,' her head was bobbing from one to the other, 'I wouldn't have said you three had the same taste at all.'

'Neither would I.'

'Duncan has a passion for fungi, don't you, dear?'

117

'Yes,' he said sheepishly. 'I am interested in fungi. In fact, it's one of the features of this place that is so interesting. These woods have some of the rarest varieties.'

'He sometimes goes out and picks them.'

'Early morning hobby of mine.'

This was a long-married couple, speaking as one, each telling part of the story. I stared back at the print and Duncan followed my gaze. 'For a fungus fanatic there's something very collectable about that print. There's something about the way she's hugging that poisonous thing.'

'I thought the same.'

And then he was staring at the print in a different way, as though he was seeing something else, something completely different, like Alice Through the Looking Glass, a scene viewed from the wrong side of the picture. 'Does she know it's dangerous, I wonder? Does she know one small bite . . .?'

'Duncan . . .?' Fiona was watching him with concern but he took no notice. 'Does she know that she's teasing, that if she opens her mouth and takes a bite – even licks it – she'll be afflicted with vomiting and hallucinations. And maybe even death.' His glance moved back to me. 'I've always found it interesting,' he said, 'the way the fly agaric is portrayed as some folk object, something fairy-like and pretty. And yet,' he said, 'they're nasty, poisonous objects. I believe death by one of these poisons is not to be recommended.'

Merryn collected up the plates. 'And by the way,' she said, 'the fungi in the venison pie tonight are guaranteed chanterelles. Dad went out at five this morning to gather them.'

'Guilty.' Duncan held up his hand. 'I admit it. There is always a huge clump over towards the Carnforths' place. I walked all the way over at five this morning and got myself a bag full.'

'It must be miles.'

118

'That's the funny thing really,' Duncan said. 'It isn't far. You see although we're the north of the town and they're the south their place is no more than two miles away as the crow flies.'

I glanced back at the print and marvelled that I had remembered the details so accurately.

I wondered if Pritchard would still be waiting as I pulled the car out of the Fairleys' drive. But the black yawned in front of me. The entire landscape was empty. I slipped the car into gear and began to descend the hill.

The mind does play strange tricks on us. We ponder points that have struck us hours ago. The evening had not quite turned out how I had expected. I had had two glasses of wine plus a gin and tonic. I was tired. I had had a long, busy day.

All these are excuses for what I saw next as I descended the rough track back to the main road.

As clearly as I had earlier seen the print against the wall I saw the child, Melanie, standing beneath a tree. She was small, with frightened, smudged eyes, a red dress with huge, white spots. Thick, fair hair. She did not move as I passed but stood and stared at me without emotion. And I was so appalled at what I had seen that I accelerated out onto the road without a backward glance.

Chapter Ten

Rosie and I managed a couple of weeks away high in the mountains of the Basque country in the north of Spain. We took the holiday with my brother Simon and it served a double purpose. I knew he had worried about me all his life, particularly now I was alone. But then Simon always had felt responsible for me. It was only now, when we looked back over the complications of our childhood, that we could see why we had always felt so threatened. We had recognised it in our father and analysed his motives even as teenagers. That was the easy bit, a man to whom intellectual dominance was paramount and any show of independence intolerable. We were not allowed our own thoughts or opinions. More subtle was the fear our mother had tried to instil in us, fear of fairy stories when we were young, dark threats of the unknown as we grew. It had been our mother who had made the attempt on our minds. So Simon and I were abnormally close. We had needed to be able to rely on each other. Lonely, insecure, we had meandered through life knowing we could depend on each other.

The holiday had been normality itself. Rosie, Simon and I had played on the beach, swam, taken sailing dinghies far out beyond the bay, walked, cycled and climbed through rough countryside. And in the evenings we had caroused the nights away at the everlasting fiestas.

Having my brother around had minimised the effect on Rosie of a holiday without her father. We did all the things a family would do, enjoyed the freedom of the bars with their tapas, and talked.

And I forgot about Melanie Carnforth.

But we had to come to the end of the holiday, fly home and return to work. And my first booked patient of the morning was Pritchard, as though he had been waiting for me to come home. It was a rude awakening.

I pressed the buzzer and waited.

I don't know how he did it. He was a heavy man. I would have thought he would have been clumsy on his feet. But although I strained to hear his approach the first I knew of his presence was the soft scrabble against the door. It was pointless calling him in. I already knew the drill. He would hesitate outside, shift his weight from one foot to the other, hover.

I stood up and pulled the door open. It shocked him so much he jerked back.

I felt a warm triumph. I had stolen a march on him. He was not invincible but a rather stupid, heavy man with a pedantic manner. I could now put him into perspective. The holiday had built my confidence. He had not followed me to the rugged terrain of the Basque country but was confined here, in this small town, folded into a forest.

'Good morning, Mr Pritchard.' I was determined not to let him intimidate me. What the hell was there to be unnerved about? A podgy, sweaty, middle-aged man with BO and high blood pressure? 'Come in, Mr Pritchard,' I said. 'Sit down.'

'Thank you, Harriet.'

It is difficult for me to describe the effect those three words had. Like a spider's web brushing your face in the dark. It was nothing. It was something. Already my bravado was evaporating. Cold fingers brushed me.

Pritchard smiled, sat down, crossed his legs and the pantomime began with the removal of the jacket, the waft of body odour, the laboured breathing, pleased expectation lighting his face. 'I believe you've had a holiday.'

I said nothing.

He pursued the subject. 'Anywhere nice?'

'Just Spain with my brother.'

'Nice,' he said. 'I wish I had a brother.'

Again I said nothing but took in every detail of him. Today's outfit was a suit, a dark green suit. Tight under the armpits, slight flares on the trousers. Tram-lined creases. There was a grease spot on his lapel and lots of tiny holes where pinholes might have been stuck. Pinholes? Had this once been a much-used wedding suit?

He slid out of the jacket. He was being careful with this suit, his best, using the chair as a coat hanger. Even draped over the chair it kept Pritchard's shape. Plump arms, a slightly hunched back. He sat and faced me.

I made a feeble attempt to regain my equilibrium. 'And how is your mother?'

He didn't answer until his sleeve had been methodically pleated up the white grub of an arm. 'I don't see what your interest is in my mother,' he said.

'She's one of my patients too,' I replied. 'As are you.' I could have added, but older, more feeble, more vulnerable.

'She's well,' he said sourly. 'She's not fallen out of bed again if that's what you're worried about.'

Maybe because you have not moved the commode, Mr Pritchard. 'Good,' I said.

He briefly fingered the frayed tie. Orange today and thin enough to have belonged in the nineteen sixties. 'I don't neglect her,' he said, 'if that's what you think.'

'No?' I wound the cuff around his arm, pumped up the bladder and listened to the slow thump of his brachial pulse. 'The drugs seem to be controlling your blood pressure remarkably well,' I said. 'Even on this low a dose.'

'That's good,' he said. 'I'm relieved. But it'll still need regular checks. Once a month.'

'The nurse can-'

'But I feel, Harriet . . .? He uncrossed his legs and crossed them again. 'I feel that it's good for me to see you

122

on a regular basis. I find you such pleasant company. I'm sure that you are as good for my blood pressure as the drugs.'

It was on the tip of my tongue to ask him then what he really wanted from me but the eyes, magnified from behind the glasses, were unblinking. I didn't want to ask him anything because his answer would prolong the consultation. I wanted him to go.

'I'm getting accustomed to seeing you on a regular basis.' At last he stood up. 'I shouldn't like these appointments to stop.' He paused and wiped beads of sweat away from his forehead before replacing his sleeve. Then his jacket. 'I look forward to them, you see. And I'm silly enough to believe that if I missed a month of your healing my blood pressure would become danger-ously high.'

To any other patient I would have pointed out the facts, that his blood pressure was not 'dangerously high', that his visits to me had no effect – therapeutic or anything else. I was doing nothing for him. The very appointments were a waste of my time, manipulated by him. I did not want them. I did not want to see him. To him I said nothing.

He held out his hand and gave me a bland smile. 'I shall see you in one month, Harriet.'

I knew that to argue would be futile. But the power-lessness was paralysing me.

Thankfully the last few weeks of the summer rolled on without further incident but in September the nights began to lengthen. There were more hours cloaked in darkness and Rosie returned to school. But now she was ten. She had moved up a class, had a new teacher. She was growing up.

She had only been back a week when she asked her first question. 'Mum,' she said, 'do some people really find girls' conversation interesting? Or are they just pretending?'

I was spooning gravy over her meal. Perhaps this is my excuse for not picking up on things.

'I find you interesting,' I said.

She was toying with her knife and fork. 'Not mums. I mean other people.'

'What sort of conversations?'

'Just about things,' she said idly. 'You know, the telly, clothes, pop music. Things.'

'Some people do seem to have the ability to relate to children better than others.'

'Oh,' she said, picked up her plate and sat down with it in front of her.

I was vaguely aware that I had given her the wrong kind of answer. But there was a reason. I had imagined she was referring to her new teacher because during the first two weeks of the new term she must have mentioned his name more than thirty times already, Jay Gordon. Mr Jay Gordon. Mr Gordon and lately, just Jay.

Two nights later she was doing her homework in her customary untidy fashion with all the books sprawled across the kitchen table when it struck me how very hard she was trying.

'What are you doing?'

'An essay,' she said, hardly looking up, 'for Mr Gordon.'

Perhaps it was the reverent way she spoke his name that alerted me. Or the pink tinge on both her cheeks. It might even have been a certain protectiveness in the way she coiled her arms around her homework book. It made me more curious than normal because she didn't want me to see it.

'What's it about?'

She looked up now. 'My family.'

'Oh.' I bristled. I was angry. How crass to set children an essay on this subject, this emotional minefield.

She chewed the top of her biro. 'It's hard to know what to write,' she said. 'I mean we've only got Tigger. And Daddy . . .' The words hung in the air, a sad epitaph.

'So what have you put?'

'Just things,' she said. 'And by the way,' she added casually, 'there's a parents' night next Wednesday so you can meet Mr Gordon then.'

'Fine,' I said.

I always feel like Alice in the tiny house when I visit a junior school. Everything's so small. It starts with the building, a toy house. The doorways look abnormally tiny, hardly big enough for a full-grown human to squeeze through. The toilets are dwarf sized. And the classrooms are filled with miniature chairs that wedge your bottom in them, small desks, small books.

I wasn't too badly off. I'm not much bigger than the average ten-year-old anyway. But as I entered I noticed that some of the other parents looked uncomfortably giantlike. I was late, a little after nine. Mine had been the last appointment of the evening, purposely.

I had pulled the car into the playground and wandered towards the entrance before I saw it. But how common a car is a blue Lada? Not unique. I should not see him every-where, behind the wheel of a common make and colour of car. And this one was not muck-splattered but clean. This reassured me. It was not his.

I carried on walking into the school and turned into Rosie's classroom. I glanced around, uncertain which was Rosie's desk until I spotted her name, clumsily drawn on a piece of card standing up on the front desk. I might have known. Keen, under the teacher's eye, close to the board. I headed in the general direction. Pairs of parents were poring over their offspring's books. All looked up as I entered. I knew none of them.

I could see Mr Gordon sitting at his desk, behind a

plastic sign which bore his name, Jay Gordon. I thought him very nondescript, with brown hair that needed trimming, and a serious face. On closer inspection I picked up that he was casually dressed in jogging pants and an open-necked shirt. I sat down in Rosie's desk and and started reading through her exercise books.

It seemed to me that while she had a flair for English with lots of ticks and 'very goods' her maths was sadly lacking. I could see depressing huge red crosses right the way through. And there were comments too. 'Don't forget your columns, Rosie' and 'I think you forgot about the decimal point'. I closed the book and glanced back at the desk.

He was still talking to the woman in the red suit and the man in jeans. I bent my head again, found an awful poem she had written and then the story she had most recently done. The opening sentence was enough to grab me.

I used to have a Dad.

He was nice but he left me and now I don't love him any more. I love someone else. It is a secret who. We don't tell anyone but he loves me like Daddy used to do. He told me that he loved me and if I was old enough he would marry me in a long white dress and lots of flowers and he told me my Mummy would cry because Mummys should cry at weddings. I think that's true.

I closed the book. Was this fantasy? Or . . .?

I glanced back at Mr Gordon, at Mr Jay Gordon. He was sitting with a different couple this time. Man in dark suit, woman in smart black trousers and a jacket. How cringingly embarrassing. They were holding hands. But Jay Gordon didn't seem in the least bit put out. In fact he was laughing with them, head thrown back.

I glanced at my watch. My appointment had been for nine-thirty. It was now nine-thirty-five. I was tired. I wished I was home. I read another page from Rosie's exercise book. No more about love this time. Instead it was meanings of words. She seemed very good on this. I glanced back at Mr Gordon again. He was still being pally with the parents. I stood up and all three turned their heads. I crossed the room towards the desk. I would have asked how long he would be but they got the message, stood up and shook hands, the three of them still laughing.

I felt such an outsider. Was this how Rosie felt at school? An outsider? Was that why she had to fantasise?

Brown eyes looked humorously into mine.

'I'm Dr Lamont,' I said abruptly; 'Rosie's mum.'

He smiled. 'I thought you probably were. You're the last parent on my list.' He scanned the room. 'I've seen all the others.' He paused before saying softly, 'Well, are you going to sit down?'

I flopped into the tiny chair and wondered irritably, Was this entire evening organised not to discuss your child's education at all but to humiliate the parent? To make them feel intruders into their children's and teachers' private world? If so it was succeeding. He was succeeding. He was calling the shots.

'Rosie's a bright child.'

'I thought her essays were good.'

'Yes,' he said. 'They are. As I say. She is a bright child. Not brilliant but bright.'

He'd got me on the defensive. Because I knew how much this faint praise would mean to her I wanted to wound him.

'She's improved just over the few weeks I've had her.'

'I don't see much evidence of that in her exercise books.'

He took no offence but again threw back his head and laughed. 'You've been studying her maths more than her English.'

It cut me down to size so I was even more prickly. 'Why did you set her that essay, Mr Gordon?' I burst out. 'She's

127

ten years old, just a very young girl. She's lost her father in abrupt circumstances. Why get such children to expose themselves and write about their half-family? You must realise that it's both difficult and embarrassing for them, sometimes upsetting.'

His brown eyes were fringed with thick, long lashes. He smiled through them. 'Are you describing your family as only half a family, Dr Lamont?'

'I . . . I . . .'

'You should read all the way through Rosie's essay, not just the first page. She's a sweet, bright kid with far more insight into her life than you give her credit for. She doesn't want to hurt you but she's bottling up a good deal of her feelings. Give her the chance. That's all I say. Give her the chance to talk. I set that essay deliberately, you know. Rosie isn't the only one in the class to come from a broken home. And for every one of those who have divorced parents there's another two who suffer misery at home, abuse from over-critical parents, sometimes drunkenness and violence. And at other times the children have all their parents' financial burdens on their shoulders. Life can be very cruel, Doctor; when you're a child. Sometimes to write about it or talk about it is a release.'

'And the bit about love?'

'Rosie's an imaginative and affectionate child,' he said.

I felt so chastened I was beginning to hate him. It seemed that this cow-eyed teacher knew more about Rosie than I did.

He stood up dismissively. 'I'd better go,' he said. 'It's late and I promised the boys that I'd get home in time to read them a story. If you don't mind.' He glanced around the room. The other parents had melted away. Ignoring me he started switching lights off. 'You aren't the only one, Doctor.'

When Rosie arrived home a week later bearing an envelope with my name on it I was not feeling terribly benevolent towards the school. I tore the envelope open, realised it was an invitation to a sixties disco for parents and was inclined to bin it.

But Rosie was watching me with a trusting expression on her face.

'It's a sixties night,' she said. 'They're having a real live band with a singer. And everyone's got to come in old fashioned gear. You know,' she said, putting her pen down. 'Mini skirts and flares and things.'

I was reminded of Pritchard's sixties flares and smiled. It was a mistake. Rosie took it as a rejection of her enthusiasm. 'You have to come, mum,' she said. 'It's raising money for the new computers.'

'On my own?'

'You could bring Neil.'

But I hesitated. Neil and I were colleagues. All right, we were also friends but I didn't want to push things too far or our easy relationship would be threatened, and then it could spill over into our work. I didn't want to invite him to a night out. At least not a sixties night at Rosie's school. It seemed too intimate, too familiar.

Rosie was eyeing me with frank hostility. 'You aren't going to come, are you, Mum? All the other mums and dads will be there, supporting the school. And my bloody mother . . .'

'Rosie,' I said sharply. 'Language.'

But she folded her books together and stood up. 'You have to come, Mum,' she said. She was close to tears. 'You have to. I promised you would.'

'Who did you promise?'

'We all promised,' she said evasively. 'Everyone in the class.'

'All right,' I said reluctantly. 'I'll tell you what. I'll ask Ruth and Arthur. If they'll go with me I'll come.'

'And if not?'

'Rosie,' I said. 'Don't ever ask the impossible.'

It was a wasted warning. Already her face had lit up. 'Three tickets,' she said, 'I'll get them tomorrow.' She threw her arms around me and for a moment I could feel her thin body, her cheek next to mine. 'All I want,' she said softly, 'is for us to be a normal family.'

It was the perfect moment to ask her who her 'secret love' was. I hugged her closely and drew breath to ask. But she jerked out of my arms, her exuberance spilling over into a funny, hopping little dance across the kitchen. 'Brilliant.'

The opportunity had passed.

And so the dance was quickening in tempo. Others were joining it. The music was loud, fast, dangerous.

Chapter Eleven

It was a warm autumn with lots of lazy, golden sunshine. With the bright colours of the trees should have come optimism, confidence, anticipation for the future. But already I was filled with foreboding. Like a drum-beat, louder, quicker, events seemed to be banging out a grim future.

I had seen nothing of Danny Small for months. Later I would learn that he had been admitted to a rehabilitation unit in yet another futile effort to cure him of his 'habit'. As usual the treatment was pointless and they discharged him with 'therapeutic' and 'maintenance' doses of methadone, theoretically monitored by urine samples. But as clean urine samples fetched fifty pence outside the clinic Danny was able to acquire all he wanted – at least nearly all he wanted.

It was never quite enough. Danny always wanted more. Just a bit more. Not very much. Just a few grammes. More.

Late one Monday morning in the middle of October he returned with his usual demands for drugs. He sauntered in, the last patient of the morning, fitted in because he had claimed a medical emergency and the receptionists, good hearted women as they were, gave him the benefit of the doubt. Because underneath we did pity these human wrecks.

And we could never afford to ignore their demands. Just in case on this one occasion they really were ill. We could never take the risk.

He still had that shifty look in his eyes, the dishevelled, evasive expression that told me nothing had changed. He still did not care whether he lived or died. As long as he got more drugs. There was no fixed amount. Just more. He didn't respond to my good morning but dropped straight into the chair.

'Dr McKinley,' he complained, 'won't give me my full dose.'

Like I said. It's never enough. They always want more. And we have to play their game.

'Why is that, Danny?'

He laughed and chewed vigorously on his gum. 'I dunno. He just says he's givin' me plenty.' He lifted his eyes with a huge effort. 'But it ain't.' His voice was flat and expressionless. It was as though he knew he was on a downward slope.

I did feel pity for him. Then.

'Would it be true to say, Doctor ...'

'I did not dislike Danny Small. He was a nuisance. That's all.'

I shrugged my shoulders. 'Would you like me to ring Dr McKinley?'

'You can if you want,' he said. 'I don't mind if you do.'

'But you know our policy here is that we don't give out methadone. All I can do is to ask Dr McKinley if he'll see you today.'

Something in Danny's demeanour was disturbing me. He was pale, dishevelled, thin. That was nothing new. It was something else. He was accepting my offer of nothing too easily. I should have realised that he had something up his sleeve. Maybe on another day I might have cottoned on to the fact that his mind was tracking in a different direction from mine. Danny was planning something while he sat there, playing meek.

We were playing a new game now – a much more dangerous game with a different set of rules: none.

But I still did not realise Danny was a danger. Not only to himself but to me.

I picked up the phone and connected with Dr McKinley.

'He'll see you at eleven o'clock,' I said finally. 'He'll want to see you producing the urine sample. If it shows problems with the levels he will give you two days' supply of methadone. If not you get nothing. Danny,' I appealed. 'It's the best I can do. Please, give it up. It's killing you. You won't survive.'

Already-dead eyes stared back at me. 'I won't survive without it.'

The hoarse whisper made me shiver. Danny Small was less than twenty years old. I couldn't see him getting the 'key of the door'.

He stood up. On my window sill I always have a plant growing. Maybe a psychologist would interpret it as a symbol of life. Bulbs in spring, violets and pansies throughout the summer, primroses in the autumn, a poinsettia at Christmas time. Maybe it was to reassure myself that normal life did exist that I took my eyes off him to look at the plant. The gesture must have annoyed him. Either that or he knew I gained pleasure from my flowers. Quite suddenly he picked up the pot and hurled it against the opposite wall.

'Fuck you,' he said and was gone.

I wasn't exactly in the mood but I had to find something for Rosie's sixties night. And the obvious place to search was the local charity shop. Not Cancer Research or Oxfam. In a rural community like this it was an animal charity which received most support.

I parked the car in my usual spot and wandered up the street, turning left at the top to the bowed windows and extravagant display of Hoof and Tail, the Animal Rights shop. There were racks of clothes, all blessed with the faintly musty air that belongs in a little-visited attic. There were dog-eared cult paperbacks, *Lady Chatterley's Lover, The Godfather, Adrian Mole*. A prayerbook. This was a glimpse of outdated fashions, rusting saucepans, plastic dishracks in the wrong colours, brown and orange, lemon and blue. And lots of olive green.

I moved to the back of the shop where a rail was swaying under the weight of clothes. Here were bobbled sweaters and lots of ethnic stuff. Crimplene. I picked out the hanger. I could remember my mother wearing a dress of Crimplene. Navy blue with white piping. I fingered the material and conjured up her face, disapproving, worrying.

I put the dress back on the rail. Whatever they did wear in the sixties I was not spending a night dressed as my mother. Instead I homed in on a tiny lime green dress, size ten. It looked relatively clean and was made of some sort of bonded crepe. A strange, slinky material, slippery as I held it against me.

'Harriet.'

I swung around. It was Pritchard. Of course. This was his stamping ground, the source of his varied wardrobe, the fusty smell, the unfashionable clothes. He moved very close to me, reached out and fingered the material.

'It has a lovely feel to it, doesn't it?'

I watched, mesmerised by the sight of the plump fingers rubbing the material.

'It is nice to see you,' he said comfortably, 'outside the surgery for once. I've been wondering where it is that you do your shopping. I find it quite pleasant to know that you and I frequent the same shops.' I said nothing and he carried on with a shared, knowing smile. 'Good value here, isn't it?'

I swallowed.

'I'm glad to see you enjoying yourself when you're off duty, doing a bit of shopping. Very nice.' His hand was on my shoulder, his face two inches away from mine. But if I moved back I would be trapped by the clothes on the rack.

Pritchard's eyes dropped to the dress I had picked out. 'What an unusual outfit to choose.' His face was sweating. 'Very fetching. And I can picture you wearing it.' His eyes were great fish balloons behind his glasses. 'Not going to a special night out, are you?'

'I . . .' I wanted to escape but he was blocking the only way through. 'I'm going to a sixties night at my daughter's school.'

His answer was quick. 'Would that be Merrivale Primary?'

The sense of intrusion was suffocating. How did he know where Rosie went to school? Like a flash I remembered the blue Lada, neatly parked, cleaned. In the school car park. Was he watching her as he watched me? Invading her privacy, as he invaded mine?

'Not there? I lied badly.'

He simply smiled and let his eyes slide down the dress I was holding. 'No? Well wherever your little girl goes to school I have to say, Harriet, I do think you'll look very nice in this. Very nice indeed. And after all, you're a single woman again now, I understand.'

It was an offensive sentence.

For a while we stood, in the musty atmosphere of the charity shop, then he blinked. 'Well, I must be going. Can't keep my mother waiting.' He moved away but only a fraction of an inch before his eyes seemed to harden. 'I hope she doesn't get taken ill again, especially at night. I would hate to have to get you out of your nice warm bed and drag you all the way out to our home. Such a lonely place, don't you think? Not somewhere a woman should be on her own. All those trees. Even I find it a bit eerie. I've often thought no one would hear you however loud you shouted if you were in need.'

He beamed at me. 'But then I'm hopeful I won't have to ask you to come out again, not at night.' He stopped looking at me and let his eyes roam along the rack. 'I can't see anything for me here today. I shall have to save my money and pop in again. By the way,' he said, 'will you still want to do that special check on my mother?' It was a challenge.

'I um . . .'

His eyes were fixed and staring now. 'You'll have to come to the house to do it,' he said. 'I can't move her.' We were both aware that he was dangling this as an invitation.

135

He knew full well how much I did not want to visit the shack in Gordon's Lane. He had picked up the feeling of vulnerable revulsion I felt for him, for his home, for his circumstances, even for his mother, and he was using it as a weapon. It was all as much part of the game as moving the commode to let her tumble to the floor. He could not have known whether or not she would hurt herself. That had not mattered. What had mattered was having the power to make her fall as he knew he had the power to lure me out to his squalid little home. *At any time.* That was why he followed me. Because he knew he pulled the strings. He could dial the number and on the nights I was on call if he used the right phrases I had no choice but to answer his summons. By using my reluctance to be drawn to Gordon's Lane he was manipulating my thoughts as well as my actions. It was the ruling that I did not have the right to refuse him anything. He was the patient, I the doctor. Pritchard had the power of the puppet master because the National Health Service gave it to him without discrimination. It was that that made me vulnerable.

I did what I could to shift my burden. 'The nurse usually . . .'

Something hard, mean and deliberate crossed Pritchard's face. 'And will she be able to check my mother for bruises?'

He was so perfectly conscious of his rights that he could flaunt it. 'I think,' he said, 'that it had better be you who comes, soon. Not some nurse.'

I waited until he had shuffled out of the shop before putting the dress back on the rack. I would find something else, something unpolluted by those hands. Further along the rail was another sixties dress, red this time, short and made of cotton. I paid up the two pounds fifty and walked back to the car park.

Déjà vu. It was hemmed in by a blue Lada. Too close for me to open the driver's door.

But this time I knew it was a deliberate gesture. And knowing the driver made it less sinister. It is the unknown which terrifies, as my mother had understood, and as Vera Carnforth knew only too well.

But I was a fool to believe I knew.

Chapter Twelve

I spoke to Rosie about the blue Lada I had seen in the school car park. I asked her who drove it. But a ten-year-old girl has scant interest in make, model or driver. She eyed me indignantly. 'I don't know which blue car you mean,' she said.

I tried to describe it and realised how all cars are essentially the same, four wheels, a colour, a vague shape, a vague length.

But the man? 'Do you know a plump man who hangs around the school? He has glasses, Rosie. Thick glasses and he always wears old clothes.'

She screwed up her face. 'What do you mean, hangs around the school?'

'Tries to talk to the children?'

She shrugged her shoulders and I gave up.

Two weeks later the riddle was solved for me.

'Lucky for me these were in fashion in the sixties.' Ruth was laughing as she turned up on the front doorstep dressed in a billowing denim smock with long, bell-shaped sleeves. She gave a little twirl before smoothing the material over her bump. 'I can't believe the rate at which the little blighter is growing.' She gave a comical, sideways look. 'Sure it's not twins, Harry?'

I took it on the chin. 'I can always arrange another scan, Ruth.'

Immediately her arms curled round her unborn child. 'I think I've had enough of those, thank you,' she said stiffly before smiling again. 'But it was nice of you to make the offer.' And she and Arthur followed me into the sitting room.

'I'm so glad you came,' I said. 'Rosie was insisting I buy a ticket but I could hardly go on my own.'

Neil, who was babysitting, as the disco was for parents only, walked in from the kitchen at that precise moment. 'I would have gone with you, Harriet.'

I winced at the hurt in his voice. I was getting the feeling that he knew I had considered asking him and had rejected the idea. But he probably didn't understand why. And I wasn't sure I would ever be able to explain to him my concern that to mix business with pleasure might ruin both. I liked things as they were, Neil a colleague, Neil a trusted family friend both to myself and to Rosie.

Sensitively Ruth tried to fill the silence. 'Don't we all look a sight, Neil? You can't possibly have wanted to come with us. Arthur, have you got your camera?'

Neil was saying nothing.

It was left to Arthur to fill the gap. 'I don't know that I want this recorded on film.' He tugged at his lapels. 'This suit used to be quite loose on me, years ago. Now look at it.' He looked as though he had been stitched into the fabric. Sausage legs, pot belly. Even the orange-flowered shirt was wrinkling tight, buttons gaping, chin spilling over the collar. He looked ten times fatter than normal. Could it ever have fitted him?

Ruth laughed again, poked his stomach and refused to give up. 'You haven't got your camera, have you, Neil? I want to compare old photos of Arthur with today's version.'

He flushed. 'Not with me.'

His shortness bordered on rudeness which at the time I still attributed to my not having invited him along. Maybe I should have asked him and had Sylvie to babysit. But she needed time away from us. Sylvie had her own life to lead.

There was an awkward lull in the conversation. I risked a swift glance at Neil and realised he was sulking, pretending to be absorbed in lining up the chess pieces with Rosie.

Again it fell to Ruth to smooth over the awkwardness. 'Where did you find your outfit, Harry? It's a bit of a wow.'

She fingered the material. 'Looks the genuine article too. Vintage fashion.'

I self-consciously tugged at the hemline. 'In a charity shop.'

'Which one?'

'The animal place,' I said. 'It's packed full of stuff.' *Visions of those soft, roly poly fingers rubbing grubby material.*

'It's brilliant,' Ruth said decisively. 'I shall have to pop along there myself and take a look. They haven't got any maternity dresses, have they?'

'I didn't see any. There were lots of baby things though.'

A change came over Ruth. Quite suddenly she looked haughty and superior. 'My baby,' she said, 'will have nothing but the best, everything new. I wouldn't want Tinker to have anything after another child. You don't know what sort that child might have been.'

'Tinker?' I queried softly.

'It's just a name.'

Arthur's arm stole around his wife's shoulders. He eyed his wife's billowing figure before turning to me. 'I've got the best of both worlds here,' he laughed. 'Jack Spratt and his wife.'

'Are you implying I've put on weight?' It was mock anger which Arthur recognised.

'I should hope you have.'

But Ruth was too happy to be down for long. The baby was everything to her now.

Rosie moved the first chess piece, a white pawn. 'Look out for Mr Gordon, Mummy,' she said. 'I know he'll be there. And I bet he'll be dancing all night. He's ever so fit.'

I recalled the jogging pants. 'I bet.'

'And I want him to know you're my Mummy and that you did come.'

'What do you mean?'

She coloured. 'He thought you probably wouldn't.'

'Oh.' I tucked the fact away, slightly insulted. He had

judged me and that had been his verdict, unlikely to let her hair down and have fun. Not for the first time I saw myself as others saw me, frumpy, humourless, a 'lady doctor' with all the connotations that evoked.

I kissed the top of Rosie's head. Surely she would have put the opinions right?

'I shall certainly tell him,' I said, 'that I am the proud mother of his star pupil.'

She giggled and nuzzled Tigger.

'Who's Mr Gordon?' There was unmistakable hostility in Neil's voice.

'He's my teacher.' A typical ten-year-old to whom school was the universe, Rosie looked surprised at his ignorance.

Neil was giving me a contemplative look and it annoyed me. I thought I could read his mind. If I could then Ruth and Arthur must be able to as well. There was no use explaining to any of them that nothing could be further from the truth. Recently and bruisingly separated I was interested in neither man in a romantic vein. Not Neil Anderson and certainly not Jay Gordon. I knew Neil was hurt. I could see pain in his eyes. If he was deluding himself that our relationship was moving towards intimacy I was sorry, and I felt awkward saying goodbye to him, conscious of the silly, little girl's dress.

Only until I got there. The school gym was full of people similarly dressed, dancing to records I must have heard in my youth. The entire room was heaving to the sound of the Beach Boys, the Hollies, the Beatles, Elvis, Cliff. The music was lively. Who could sit down? Not us. Ruth and I threw our bags down on the nearest chair and gyrated with the best of them. They were lively, optimistic records, from a confident, hopeful era. The music embodied all that was missing from today. It was full of naive confidence and sentimental ballads about love at a bus stop, about flowers and hope, peace and dreams. I had been nine years old when the sixties had ended yet I was filled with nostalgia for those days because there was none of the hopelessness of today's pop music, Rap, House, Drum 'n' Bass. The lyrics seemed to explore happiness, not crime, not defeat and not hopelessness. I stopped feeling self-conscious about my short skirt. We were all wearing them. And Arthur looked just like all the other men. They had all been poured into old suits, double breasted with flared trousers. They had kept their sixties memories but had lost their sixties waist-lines.

Except the lithe Mr Gordon. He was contorting in the centre of a small ring of clapping people, bending over backwards so far I thought he would topple. I smiled at him. The peace and love was reaching me too. He was simply Rosie's teacher. He waved back at me and grinned before crossing the room.

'Dr Lamont,' he shouted.

'Mr Gordon,' I shouted back.

'Rosie was right.'

'Sorry?'

'You came.'

'Of course.' If the music had not been so loud I would have added sarcastic comments, that doctors didn't have two heads, that I didn't always have a stethoscope wound around my neck. But the music was too loud for anything but shrugs and smiles.

And Jay Gordon grinned again. 'So let's dance.'

Now Ruth, Arthur, myself and Jay Gordon danced in a foursome in long forgotten jerks and jigs, occasionally twirling round or slapping our hands, stamping our feet, but always smiling. I smiled a lot that evening.

I could feel the muscles ache because they had atrophied. And the smiling seemed to bring genuine happiness. Maybe it was the dancing, a vigorous, happy pursuit. Maybe it was the music. But I suddenly realised I was honestly happy and I didn't care about Robin any more. I fondly believed that I was at last shaking off the New Year's

142

ill omens. Next year would be better. And to myself I whispered the phrase a second time. Next year will be better. *Because now I am happy.*

These are tempting, dangerous words even to whisper.

At ten the music stopped abruptly and Jay excused himself, saying he had to help with the supper. He vanished through a door, a wide hatch was thrown open and we all queued along the side of the hall for a meat pie supper on a paper plate. The pie looked about as appetising as an old shoe but I was hungry enough to eat even that. It was an unfamiliar feeling. I queued behind Ruth and watched her pick one up.

And then I watched her face change as she met the fish balloon eyes of the server. Ruth snatched the plate from him and moved away before waiting for me to catch her up.

I too held out my hand for a plate from Pritchard. He bent forward from the waist, leaning right over the counter. 'Hello, Harriet,' he said softly. 'I wondered if this was why you were buying the dress.' His eyes stroked my form. 'But you're not wearing it, are you? Still. I do like the one you're wearing, though not as much.'

He gave one of his bland smiles. 'I've been watching you dancing. Enjoying it, weren't you? You're really very graceful. But then you're small. Not much bigger than a child yourself.' He was still grasping the plate.

What was he doing here? Why did he hang around Merrivale School? He could not be a teacher, surely?

Dazed I wandered back to the table and sat down between Ruth and Arthur. It seemed that Ruth was bothered by Pritchard too. She wasn't touching her pie but staring back at him.

'Harriet,' she said slowly. 'Do you know that man?'

'Sort of,' I said. 'He's a patient.'

'But you don't like him,' she said, 'do you?'

'That's an understatement. He gives me the creeps.' But even then I was troubled by the confession, especially to

143

another of my patients. It was my business to treat them. Not to like them or dislike them. And certainly not to fear them. They had never told us at medical school how to deal with the fear of a patient. Surely a vet is finished the moment he begins to fear vicious dogs? Then was the same true of a doctor, or a psychiatrist? Once we fear our patients have we lost all our power?

And I did. I feared both Anthony Pritchard and Danny Small but for different reasons. Danny because I knew he would do *anything* for drugs, while Pritchard was an unknown. I neither knew his motives nor his objectives. I didn't know why he kept coming to see me. And it was the unknown that I feared so much.

Ruth was speaking at my elbow. 'Why don't you like him?'

'I don't know,' I said. 'Instinct?'

She gave a satisfied little humph. 'So even you believe in instinct?'

'A bit too much,' I admitted, 'for a scientific person. Why?'

Her hand grasped my arm. 'And you have an instinct about that man?'

'Ruth,' Arthur remonstrated. 'Don't.' He was annoyed with her.

She quelled him with a look. 'We'll have a child of our own soon, Arthur,' she said fiercely. 'And Tinker may be a daughter. Do you want the same thing to happen to her as happened to that poor child?'

My ears were tingling. I knew they were talking about Melanie Carnforth.

Arthur was looking lightning-struck. 'But we don't know what happened, Ruth,' he said. 'No one knows.'

'Oh yes we do.' There was a certain viciousness in Ruth's voice. 'I went to the library and found all the old newspaper articles. She disappeared, almost certainly murdered. End of story. A great big blank and a killer is still on the loose.

144

How would you feel if that was your daughter who had disappeared? Our precious, precious child? And now we find him in a school?'

Arthur muttered something, picked the glasses up and left to queue for the bar.

Ruth leaned towards me. 'Why do you think you have an instinct about that man?'

My mind flashed, the odd story about his father, the malevolent prank he had played on his mother, the insinuating way he intruded.

Something.

'Because,' I said finally, 'I can picture him doing it.'

And I could. I could see it, firstly him getting close to the child, brushing against her, as he did with me, rubbing her with his his fat, roly poly fingers, with that strange dysfunctional look in his eyes, just the way he looked at me.

'Exactly.' She glanced around the hall to check no one was eavesdropping. 'You know that story you were asking about?' She spoke quickly, the words tumbling out, slightly muddled. 'The little girl.'

I nodded.

'You know I said I thought they'd got the right man all along? That he was arrested but not charged?' Ruth said. 'But we all knew he was guilty. Evidence pointed to him.' She was staring at Pritchard. 'What I want to know is,' she said, 'what is that man doing hanging round a school?'

I caught her feeling of foreboding. 'He shouldn't be allowed here.'

'Exactly. He has no excuse. He hasn't got children, here at the school, has he?' Unconsciously her hands stole around her bump.

'No. He isn't married.'

'Does he work here, do you think?'

'I don't know.'

Ruth gave me a hard stare. 'Well, if my daughter was a pupil I'd sure as hell want to know what a little shit like him

145

was doing here. And if he does work here I bet he hasn't told them he was questioned in connection with the disappearance of that poor child. Harriet,' she said, 'we have an obligation to report this to the authorities.'

I struggled to be impartial. 'But what evidence was there against him?'

'They found the little girl's dress along the road where he lives. There's only one house along that road, Harriet.' Ruth's eyes were luminous dark pools as she spoke. They reminded me of the twin heron pools, the bridge of her nose the causeway. I felt sick.

'Why wasn't he charged?'

'There was no more evidence. He'd been too clever for them. And they never found the body. The poor little thing.'

The rest of the evening passed in a haze. I know I danced a couple of times with Jay Gordon but I could not enjoy the music as I had before and he seemed disappointed. I tried to ask him by eye movements and shouting what Pritchard was doing here but the music was too loud. He simply shook his head and grinned. It didn't help that Pritchard had parked himself on the edge of the dance floor, set apart from the other groups of watchers. And every time I glanced across at him I could tell he was watching me.

He watched only me. I never saw his head turn away once.

A little after midnight, accompanied by groans of disappointment, the music finally stopped. The lights went on and we all saw ourselves for what we were, thirty somethings who had been playing the sweet game of being teenagers all over again. I felt tired.

Jay Gordon crossed the floor A bouncing step, no paunch yet. Black jeans and an open-necked shirt. 'What was it you were trying to ask me?'

I spotted Pritchard on the other side of the hall, holding out a black, plastic bin liner. Someone was dropping paper cups into it, and the remains of the pies.

'That man,' I said. 'Who is he?'

'Pritchard?'

I knew he was curious about the tone in my voice. 'He works here. He's the sort of janitor. Why?' He laughed awkwardly. 'What's the problem? Mrs Lamont, Harriet, I can assure you, there's no harm in him.'

But I could fill in things Jay Gordon obviously knew nothing about. I knew that he watched Rosie as he watched me. He had known that she was my daughter and he had known she was at Merrivale Primary. He had got away with it once. The police had been close but the law had protected him. The burden of proof had been too light.

And now he was close to my daughter.

Chapter Thirteen

I know the way these people work. They deliberately take jobs to be near children. They gain their trust and their friendship. The children hardly notice them they are so familiar. And then when they have selected a child, a vulnerable child, they stalk it as a cheetah stalks a zebra, waiting for that child to be isolated from the herd. They derive satisfaction as much from the watching and dirty fantasies as from the act itself. They watch children.

Instinct told me Pritchard was such a man. Instinct told me I must act. But how? I could alert the authorities. But on suspicion alone?

I could almost hear their scepticism. 'So, Doctor, you have this *suspicion?*'

It was no good. There had been no proof. I knew where the proof lay, with the body of Melanie Carnforth. Find that and you will have your proof. So where was it? They must have searched the woods. Acres of trees, covering the sides of the hill as far as the eyes could see, stretching right round the eastern side of the town. It was too big.

I had to talk to someone. I thought Neil would be ideal. I thought he would give the subject the gravity it demanded. Instead he seemed irritated. Maybe he had not yet forgiven me for not asking him to the sixties night.

'Why are you so interested in a murder that happened so long ago?'

'So you do think Melanie was murdered?'

'Yes I do,' he said reluctantly. 'It stands to reason. The child is dead, Harriet. She must be. And if she isn't dead she would have been sixteen years old by now.'

'They have to find her body,' I said.

'Why?' he said impatiently. 'What on earth's the point of dragging the whole thing up again? Let the poor child rest.'

'You don't understand, Neil. The innocent are still under a cloud. And the guilty can reoffend. And Vera Carnforth still doesn't know what happened to her granddaughter.'

'And what good will it do if she does know?'

'You sound as though you don't care that a child murderer is walking free.'

'Oh.' Neil was exasperated. 'You're being completely over the top.'

'But Pritchard,' I insisted. 'He works at the school,' I said. 'Rosie's school. And that is typical of these types. They get near to children through their job. I'd have thought you'd have cared about Rosie.'

Neil's face softened. 'I do, Harry,' he said. 'Of course I do. But she isn't in any danger. Even if Pritchard really was the person who abducted and killed Melanie nothing has happened for ten years. There hasn't even been a report of an attempted abduction. If Pritchard's innocent you're dragging up an old case for nothing.'

I felt cruel then, cruel and lonely because I knew I would do anything to make him see. 'So what would you have done if you had made the same discovery, that a suspected child killer was working at Sandy's school when he was ten years old?'

'I'd have done nothing,' Neil said viciously. 'Suspicion is not the same as guilt. If there had been hard and fast evidence Pritchard would have been charged and convicted.'

'Without a body?'

'Well that makes it more difficult.'

'Sure of his innocence, are you, Neil? Sure enough to risk Rosie vanishing in the same way?'

A shadow moved across his face. 'Maybe,' he said, 'you'd better have a word with the headmaster. But be careful. You're a doctor, the man's own doctor. You shouldn't forget that position of privilege and responsibility. You have a clear duty towards your patient which you're breaching now. All you're talking about is "hunches". Doctors don't work on hunches, Harriet. Even what you're saying is slanderous. If word got out – you know how the newspapers treat such people. And you've no proof. Just hunches, instincts and silly superstitions.'

The headmaster was not convinced. I could see it in his pale eyes, in the tightening of his lips, in the way he fiddled with his pencil.

'I don't quite understand what you want me to do.'

Patiently I explained and watched his dislike for me grow.

'Dr Lamont,' he said finally. 'We knew that Mr Pritchard was questioned over the missing little girl. He was quite open about it when he applied for the job. But he was never formally charged.'

'He was questioned.'

'I expect many people were questioned.'

I conceded the point and he stood up. 'Well, Dr Lamont. I'm very grateful to you for bringing this to my attention. But as I'm sure you know, in this country one is innocent until proved guilty. He wasn't even charged. From what you say the only evidence was the fact that the child's dress was found in his road.'

'He is the only person who lives up that road.'

'Lives, yes. Anyone could walk up that road. We must not let our prejudices stand in the way of appointing our staff, particularly in the education service.'

I was feeling desperate. 'I don't know all the evidence against him,' I said sharply. 'I am not privy to police files.'

'But the police are. If there was anything concrete they would have charged him.' He shook my hand. 'Thank you so much for bringing this matter to my attention. We will be vigilant.'

'And what action will you take?'

I knew the answer. None. Pritchard was to be left roaming around a primary school because there was no proof.

But I was a mother. I had a duty to my daughter. I had to protect her. Stuff proof. Suspicion was enough for me.

I asked Rosie if she knew Anthony Pritchard.

'Piggy Pritch?' She smothered a giggle with her palm. 'Everyone knows him. He's dead peculiar.'

I stopped in my tracks. 'How peculiar? What does he do?'

Rosie wasn't even looking at me but at the television. 'He asked me if I wanted a lift home one day.'

I could picture it clearly, the blue car sliding insinuatingly close to the kerb, the window dropping, the 'friendly' offer to a child to take them home. Only he wouldn't.

'You mustn't get in the car. Not ever.'

'I wouldn't,' she said. 'He's a right weirdo.'

I was a tiny bit reassured then. Children knew. Their instincts told them Pritchard was strange. No one was telling *them* to scoff at instinct. They knew he was not to be trusted.

'Does he ever make approaches to you?'

She was lolling across the sofa, her eyes following the soap, the cat nestled against her, purring softly. 'What do you mean approaches?' Her eyes briefly left the TV screen.

'Does he talk to you? Try and get you on your own?'

'I'd run,' she said, still giggling. 'The fat thing wouldn't catch me.'

I was tempted to shake her. 'Rosie,' I said. 'This is important. Does he ever approach you?'

'He sometimes asks if we want sweets.'

'For what?' I said. 'What does he want when he offers you sweets?'

She hunched her shoulders in a definite don't-know. 'I never take them,' she said. 'They're always stuck together. Yuck.'

But I knew I must warn her. 'Rosie,' I urged, 'have nothing to do with him. If he tries to get you to go somewhere with him, don't go. Don't speak to him. Don't take his sweets.'

'Why?'

'I think,' I said, 'that he's one of those people who tries to get too close to children.'

But I could tell I had failed to alert her. She looked wholly unconcerned. The credits flashed up with the signature tune and she sat up. 'Can I go out to play now?'

The dancing patients' jig was changing. Slowing, quickening then slowing again and it had changed to a minor key. The patients were taking odd lunges at me. Danny had become strange. Pritchard still came for his monthly blood pressure check. Vera Carnforth had not been near the surgery for months and I felt that in her eyes I had let her down. She had trusted me, the doctor, and twice I had let her down. Reuben had died despite me and I had failed to keep my promise. 'Help me, Doctor. Help me.' But I hadn't. I had done nothing.

Even my surgery had lost that comfortable, homely look. The walls were permanently stained from the damp soil from my flowerpot. The carpet too was stained and there remained an odd musty smell which reminded me of graveyard earth. When Fern brought my coffee in a couple of mornings later she gave a sniff followed by a tut of disapproval. 'It'll have to be decorated, Harriet. And the carpet cleaned.'

'I know. But when? It's always in use.'

We both stared around the scarred room and shared the same anger.

'Drug addicts,' she said, then brightened. 'I know,' she said. 'Dr Anderson's on holiday again in a couple of weeks' time. Why don't you move in there?'

'Can you arrange for the handyman to come in then? And while he's at it,' I said, 'I think I'll go for a change of colour.'

Her face brightened. 'I'll get some shade cards. What about pink?'

I made a face.

'Don't you worry about a thing. You choose your colour scheme and I'll arrange everything.'

'Not pink though,' I warned.

She left me cheered. With my room decorated in warm, clean colours, things, I thought, would seem more normal.

When Jay Gordon rang two days later to ask me out for a drink I accepted, feeling more cheerful than I had since the sixties night.

But Pritchard was inching closer. I might forget him for a moment but he had not forgotten me.

It was a Thursday night in November, a night which followed a rainy, grey day. Surgery had been busy and I was on call, hopping around the house when the message appeared on my pager.

Amelia Pritchard, aged 84, Gordon's Lane, vomiting all day.

The telephone number followed. I read it twice through. I knew what he was doing. He was daring me, dancing round me, teasing and challenging. Lunging.

But I wasn't frightened now. At least not for myself. I wasn't a child. Therefore I thought he was no threat to me. So bravely I believed I could use these enforced encounters to my advantage. I could learn things about him, I reasoned. And who better to inform against him than his mother?

And so when I read the message I welcomed the chance to observe Anthony Pritchard at close quarters. For sometimes confrontation can be a relief.

'Grasp the nettle, child,' my mother had urged while my father had stared silently. Only later I had realised why he could say nothing. He did not want me educated. Dominance came with superiority. If I gained a degree he would lose status. So he would chip at my confidence with a chisel while my mother used me as her weapon against him.

I dialled the number.

He picked the other end up straight away.

'What seems to be the trouble, Mr Pritchard?'

Typically he didn't tell me. It was all part of the menace, you see. He knew my mind would torture out the details. 'I wonder if you'd come and take another look at my mother.'

I could hear rain spilling down the gutters and pictured a torrent flushing down Gordon's Lane. 'What's the matter with her?'

'She won't stop being sick.' There was a note of triumph which he was not bothering to conceal.

'How long has she been vomiting for?'

'Nigh on two days. She's kept nothing down. And now her mind's wandering.'

I understood then. Pritchard knew enough about medicine to force me to drive along that lonely lane. Someone who vomits is usually suffering from a minor illness but superimpose age and a wandering mind and alarm bells would ring in the head of any doctor. I had no option.

I knocked on Sylvie's bedroom door, told her to keep the house locked, to let no one in, to guard Rosie. I told her where I was going. I told her when I would be back.

Then I got into my car and drove.

I had been right about the lane. Rivulets poured along the twin furrows. Droplets as big as marbles beat a tattoo on the car windscreen as the wiper blades sliced across my vision, diverting the cascade.

I put the radio on, craving the tranquillity of Chopin or Schubert. But tonight there was no music, only *Gardeners'*

Question Time. Questions about pruning and bulbs for a long distant spring. I was disappointed. Music helped me not to think. So my mind was too busy as I drove.

I would examine the old lady, test her son's story and remove her to a place of safety if it was necessary. I had a duty to protect her. At the time I believed that all the malevolence was in the son. Although I had recognised the cottage as having some sort of atmosphere I forgot that sometimes sons could take after their mothers or fathers. Pritchard's father had been violent and I was certain he had been murdered, either by Pritchard, even though he had only been a small child, or his mother. The GP had pointed me in the right direction.

Where had Pritchard hidden Melanie's body?

'This is silly, Harriet.' My voice echoed round the car, normal, disapproving. Maybe I should have asked for police protection. But I knew they would have laughed. 'What, a harmless old man and a sick old lady? This is no drug addict, Doctor. There is no threat.'

I sliced across the causeway, looking both left and right into the Heron Pool. No moon reflections there tonight. It was as dark and cold as the grave. Splashes of rain bounced across the surface, picked out by my car headlights.

I turned left and headed along the avenue underneath the bowing hedge until I found the glimmering lights of the tin shack. His Lada was standing outside as though it had decided to declare itself. No subterfuge now. We were in the open. I switched off the engine, turned off the headlights, paddled through the yard and banged on the door.

Immediately I knew he was aware of my suspicions.

For the first time he was formal. 'Good evening, Dr Lamont.' It was a distancing from friendship. The headmaster must have said something. Pritchard was no longer my uncomfortable friend.

And I felt as threatened by his distance as I had recently

been by his forced and uninvited intimacy. So I was brusque. 'Where is she?'

I hadn't needed to ask. From the bedroom I could hear the unmistakable sound of retching. I knew that sound. There is vomiting and there is the sound of an empty stomach heaving. I knew she was violently ill. But even I was unprepared for the hollow cheeks, the exhaustion, the skin so deprived of moisture it lifted between my fingers in a pleat and stayed there.

Her eyes were glazed. She did not know me.

'How long has she been like this?'

'A day or two.' Pritchard was calm. Maybe the tricks were no longer any fun on his mother. Maybe she was just too weak, too old, too decrepit. Or maybe she was simply in the way.

'Has she ever vomited like this before?'

'No.'

'Has there been any blood in the vomit?'

'No.'

'Did she eat something?'

An imperceptible pause. 'I'm not here for most of the day. I work.'

I gave the old lady a quick examination. Stomach rigid, desiccated skin, coated tongue.

Surely the police had interviewed her too? Surely ten years ago she had given or not given her son an alibi? Maybe there was the answer. Maybe she had. Now she might be dying she might yearn to tell the truth. I might not be given another opportunity.

I lifted the phone and called an ambulance. I had to answer the usual questions, justify the use of siren and blue light at this late hour. But the old lady was still conscious and I tipped some of the vomit from the inappropriate washing up bowl into a specimen pot. I would send it for analysis.

This vomiting could kill her. So what had caused it?

Pritchard's eyes were hostile. 'What are you doing that for?' Sometimes lies can be justified. 'I think there may be blood in it.'

'So what?' He was unsympathetic.

'It could help with diagnosis.'

His face was too close to mine. 'So what is the diagnosis?' There was mockery in his voice now. He was challenging my knowledge.

I had my suspicions, although I had no intention of telling him what they were: that she was now dying in exactly the same manner as her husband had died years ago.

Doctors can lie too. 'At the moment I'm wondering whether your mother might have a bleeding gastric ulcer.'

Pritchard was unimpressed. 'I've never heard her complain.'

'It could have happened quite suddenly.'

His eyes dropped to the shrunken figure on the bed. 'Have you pain, mother?'

She could hardly bear to look at him but dropped her head back into the bowl, groaning.

I wanted to be alone with the old lady. 'You'd better pack some clothes,' I said. 'And then go and watch for the ambulance.'

I felt a bully questioning the old woman. 'Amelia,' I whispered. 'Did you give your son an alibi? Did he kill Melanie Carnforth?' Her eyes fluttered open. 'Tell me,' I urged. 'You're very ill. You mustn't keep secrets now.'

I knew she had heard me. Her eyes might be dull and lifeless but I knew she could understand all that I was saying. I would use any weapon against him. 'You are a Christian,' I hissed. 'You must tell me.' I flung all on my last throw. 'This might be your last chance to tell the truth.'

Her head rolled across the pillow and she retched again. One claw hand shot out and gripped me. 'You're right. It was murder.' At last. I had known it. My instinct had told me right. He had killed her. I had found the murderer of Melanie Carnforth. The old lady would confess all now.

I could hear Pritchard moving in the room beyond. 'Tell me,' I ordered.

'I fed him.' Her eyes bored into me. We were connected, soul to soul. 'The Destroying Angel. The Destroying Angel.' She cackled. 'The Angel Destroys.'

And yet my mind was so focused on Melanie Carnforth I was not listening. Instead I was busy connecting. My mind was filled with pity for the little girl. The angel had been destroyed.

'Melanie?' I asked eagerly.

For one second her mind was as lucid as mine. 'Not Melanie,' she said quite clearly. 'Rupert, my husband.'

Chapter Fourteen

In the morning I rang the hospital and learnt that Amelia Pritchard had died two hours after admission. There was to be a post mortem.

The pathologist was a friend of mine, an old mate from the same medical school. He was perfectly frank with me. 'I have to tell you, Harry,' he said, 'not only can I not find a cause of death but I can find no real reason for the vomiting.'

Science may have most answers but not all. Never all. 'So what next?'

'I've sent some samples off to toxicology,' he said, 'and to biochemistry. We wondered whether uraemia might be the cause of her vomiting.'

'But vomiting causes uraemia,' I said. 'So you'll find that anyway.'

'Yeah,' he said casually. 'True.'

'I don't suppose she could have been poisoned?'

'Got anything in mind?'

'No.'

He gave a coughing laugh. 'Well,' he said. 'If you think of anything.'

I mailed the specimen myself and filled out the form. Sometimes you have to keep suspicions to yourself.

It was to be a bad week. Two nights later I left the surgery at a little after seven both tired and irritable. Rosie was having tea with a friend and I was looking forward to getting home. Rain had sharpened to frost by the time I left in pitch darkness through the back exit. Vandals had smashed the lamp and we had not yet replaced the bulb. We were at a disadvantage. Though our patients' car park was conveniently round the front of the building, well lit and public, staff cars were parked round the back. It was a remote patch of land overlooked by a derelict factory that had recently been bought for development. Like all patches of dereliction many people had a use for it, drug addicts, 'fences' with goods to sell, courting couples, dog owners.

I don't know where Danny had been hidden. I was unaware anyone was there until I felt an arm smash into my back and my face kiss the car window.

'Hand us your bag.'

I handed him my handbag. Five pounds cash and my credit cards. My anger bubbled away.

'Don't look at me.' I didn't need to. I knew it was Danny. Keep calm. This was something they did teach us at medical school. Keep calm. Take the heat out of the situation. Avoid eye contact and confrontation. And above all keep calm.

I could hear him rummaging through my bag and risked a peep. That was how I saw the knife. Don't think what he could do with that knife.

My bag dropped to the floor.

'There's bugger all in here.'

My face was pushed harder against the window of my car. Through it I could see my Gladstone bag on the passenger seat. So could Danny.

'Open the door.'

I moved my hand towards the handle. He wasn't that stoned. As my fingers pulled the handle he stopped me by pricking the knife against my neck. 'I don't want the alarm to go off.'

Cold steel has a curious scent to it. Not just the steel, something else, metallic and pungent. My own fear? Or was it anger? Because they have a scent too.

The blade had been polished clean. By the light of frosty stars it shone. Danny must have cleaned it. For me?

I was afraid of that knife. In a determined hand it could cut as deep as a scalpel. Keep calm.

'Where's your keys?'

'In my bag.' I was tempted to add his name. 'Danny.' Would it have helped or not? I could not risk it. He was too unstable. The wrong word at the wrong time could cost me. Visions of Rosie flashed through my mind and the word *if*... just *if*... What would happen to her *if*...?

Robin? Janina? Help my child. Protect her.

A vision of a child hugging a poisonous toadstool.

This was my fear, deep and paralysing. I was tempted to beg. On my knees. On behalf of my child I wanted to beg. Leave me alone. Don't kill me. Please.

She needs me. She is innocent. She does not know the danger.

My bag was shoved into my back. 'I said, find your keys.'

I opened my bag and for a moment this ordinary activity calmed me. I always carried a large, deep bag. And I never could find my keys, because they always dropped to the bottom, hiding behind my purse or slipping inside my cheque book, tangling with my comb or sliding through the lining.

My fingers scrabbled blindly, hunting for the sharp, irregular shapes. Delay. They appeared in my hand as though by magic. I pressed the electronic key, tugged the door open and Danny reached over me to grab my doctor's bag.

It had been bought by a proud mother even though I had warned her it was drawing attention to my profession. That, of course, was why she had bought it. To rub it in, revenge herself finally on her husband. It had been a venomous gift, heavy with years of suppressed spite. Even now simply to carry it made me uncomfortable. It was as though she was with me.

And now Danny had it and was scrabbling around inside it. 'What's this?' He had found something. He held it up in front of the car courtesy light.

I risked a glimpse and was tempted to laugh hysterically. He'd homed in on a ten millilitre ampoule of potassium

161

chloride, KCl. Main line that, Danny Boy, and you'll be off doctors' lists for ever and onto someone else's. And he'll visit you at night, whether you ask him to or not.

With the familiar object my fear receded. My confidence was returning. Perhaps he would not kill me or maim me. Maybe he only wanted the usual. Money, drugs. *He must not know I recognised him.*

'Potassium,' I said. 'Potassium chloride. We use it . . .'

He knew what it was. Drug addicts are knowledgeable. They are also cunning. With a grunt he flung it across the floor. I heard it smash. Tinkle tinkle.

'Great.' He'd found something else.

I risked another peep beneath my elbow.

He'd found a bottle of Temgesic. A patient had returned them. They hadn't helped her sleep. I'd dropped them into my bag without thinking. To me they were returned drugs, a waste product. To Danny they were a lifeline.

He pocketed them before delving back into my bag like a lion returning to a scavenged carcase and I was left cursing myself for the Temgesic.

We had had a talk a few months ago from a Police Constable Harper with a 'special interest' in drugs. He had come to give us a code of conduct, helpful advice in the care of drugs. Already I knew he would sneer.

'So you had a bottle of Temgesic in your possession?' And he would give a sad shake of his large head. 'And you wonder why they keep targeting you doctors. They go for your cars, your surgeries, your homes. You're your own worst enemies, Doctor. We've told you before. Don't carry drugs.'

Useless to protest that we were doctors. We had to carry drugs. They were life savers, sometimes.

Danny was still grunting like a pig foraging for truffles. He fished out another trophy. Adrenaline this time. More grunts. He'd found some Prozac now and I almost rubbed my hands. I couldn't have prescribed better myself. I was feeling brave now. Forgetting about the knife. Swallow them whole, Danny Boy, the ruddy lot. Then sit back and wait for them to take effect.

He stuffed them into his pocket. He'd come to the bottom. He threw the bag down and pressed the knife against me, right through my coat, into my blouse. I heard material tearing, felt the prick of the knife. I felt bile well up in the back of my throat.

Danny had been disappointed.

He would take revenge on me.

I wanted to plead again. 'Please . . .' For Rosie I tried to beg. 'Please.'

Danny snarled into the back of my neck. 'I know where you live, Doctor. And I know where your little girl goes to school. That's not all I know. I know you're not there at the gates to meet her. You tell anyone about this and I'll pick her up one day. Instead of the slimy old goat in the Lada it'll be cousin Danny with a nice little happy pill for her to try.'

Chapter Fifteen

PC Harper was reproachful when he finally arrived. Typical. Prang another car and they appear as if by magic. Summon them to an assault and robbery and they ignore you. And when they do come there's no blue light or comforting siren. Just a marked car and a couple of reluctant coppers.

'I did warn you,' he said sadly. 'I did tell you to take care.'

I had my defences ready. 'I thought I'd be safe just walking from the surgery to the car park.'

'Unlit?' he said.

'The light had been vandalised.' I was in a defensive, truculent mood. I had not stood up to Danny so my anger was turning inwards, curling at the edges. My aggression was focused on the police. Why could they not control this epidemic of pushers, robbers' burglars? Why didn't they do something? Protect us? Anything?

But they had never charged Pritchard, had they?

So there was resentment in my voice as I answered. 'I did explain before. We have to carry drugs. We're doctors.' I risked sarcasm. 'Sometimes we save lives.'

PC Harper gave a slow, deliberate blink. 'Let's get our priorities right,' he said slowly. 'First of all, do you need a doctor, Doctor?' I could have sworn there was a hint of malice, of mockery in the repetitive phrase.

'No,' I said savagely. 'I don't need a doctor, thank you.'

I'd taken a peep at my injury in the surgery toilet. An elastoplast would have been overkill. However terrifying it had seemed at the time I'd known rose thorns do more damage than Danny's knife. What troubled me was not what he *had* done but what he *might* have done.

'OK.' Harper took out his note pad with an air of resignation. 'So what's gone?' I started with the five pounds.

He looked up briefly. 'And?'

'Adrenaline, Prozac and Temgesic.'

I was shrinking by the minute. Harper might have known that adrenaline would be normal emergency treatment and Prozac could be swallowed by the lorry load before having any ill effects. At a guess its street value was negligible. But Temgesic?

'He hit lucky then, didn't he?'

I nodded sheepishly. 'They were drugs returned by a patient.'

'Get many of those do you, Doctor?'

'It happens occasionally.'

He stopped writing to look at me. 'And you just stuff them in the bottom of your bag?' It was a kindergarten telling off.

I made an attempt to divert his thoughts. 'I'm concerned about the threats he made against my daughter.'

Harper dismissed them with a wave of his hand.

'They make these threats,' he said. 'They rarely carry them out.'

I was unconvinced. 'With someone like him,' I said, 'who knows? He said he knew which school she was at. He said he knew I wasn't always there to meet her. I'm frightened for her.' Even I had the good sense not to drag Pritchard's name in at this stage.

Harper looked paternalistic. 'I should arrange for her to go home with a friend on the days you can't be there. She'll probably like that.' He obviously didn't have kids of his own. Rosie liked to flop, zombie-like, in front of the TV for an hour at least before she reverted to human form.

Harper wrote something carefully in his notebook before looking up. 'And you say you're sure you know who it was?'

I nodded.

'Then you won't mind making an identification at the station?' He smiled. 'We've a sort of rogues' gallery.' It was a hugely unfunny joke.

'I'd like to go home now.' I wished I didn't sound so much like a child excusing herself from class.

Harper was implacable. 'Tomorrow then,' he said.

'I'll call in the morning, after surgery.'

I was glad to get home, glad Rosie did not seem to notice I was late picking her up and that I was disturbed. We ate together quietly. I was tempted to break a rule and switch the TV on during the meal to distract her. I knew I must look strange. Maybe she did pick something up. As soon as tea was over she disappeared upstairs to take a bath.

In the silence I could think about it. As I drank my coffee I noted with almost clinical detachment that my fingers were trembling, my mouth dry. I felt cold. All the physical signs of shock were there. I must have sat for half an hour without moving. I heard Rosie's bath water drain down the plug, her CD player thud out some music. I still didn't move. My initial anger had been inconveniently replaced by the circular question, What if?

I don't know how much longer I would have sat there had I not been disturbed by a knock. I shook myself, but still seemed unable to move. The knock came again. It was followed by a voice. 'Harry. Hello?'

Rosie shot into the lounge like an excited puppy. 'It's Daddy. Mum, It's Daddy.'

All the pent up love spilt out as she raced across the room, flung open the door and hurled herself into Robin's arms.

He looked past her uneasily. 'I heard about . . .'

'How?'

'Fern gave me a ring,' he said. 'She was concerned.' For a moment I was angry with Fern for her interference. That was before it hit me.

Old habits die hard. And who else would she ring?

It must have seemed natural for her to ring Robin. It was so logical. Robin loved vulnerability, women in trouble.

166

And now his ex-wife and daughter needed him.

'We *are* still married,' he said reproachfully, 'just.'

'Only because you won't send the papers back.'

He gave me one of his beseeching smiles. 'I thought I could put Rosie to bed for you.'

So Rosie was part of the plot.

'You could read me a story,' she said, adding, 'Daddy,' in a hesitant, questioning voice.

He kissed the top of her head. 'So I could.'

And before I could say anything they had climbed the stairs together. From her bedroom I could hear them giggling.

I sat back on the sofa. He was her father. What harm could it do? None to her, but I was still susceptible and tonight especially vulnerable. Fear could evaporate as quickly as it had appeared. I did not want to be alone. I wanted him to stay and I was not above feminine wiles.

I peeped at myself in the mirror, made a quick swipe with a lipstick, fingers through hair. Lamp switched on, main lights off. I felt nervous, almost too nervous to pull the cork from a bottle of wine.

I was on my second glass by the time he returned. I liked the way he knocked on the door and stood, while the light caught his blond hair. Maybe I had grown used to the inhabitants of this house being myself and Rosie. He looked enormous. 'Rosie's almost asleep,' he said softly.

I smiled invitingly at him. 'Good.'

He cleared his throat nervously. 'That wouldn't be wine, would it?'

I held out the bottle. 'Want some?'

'I'll just get a glass.'

He dived into the kitchen and was back in a long blink, closing the door deliberately. It evoked memories of sexy evenings on the sofa. It seemed years ago.

Robin poured himself a glass of wine and settled down beside me on the sofa. 'It's good to be back.'

It was not a neutral statement. 'You aren't back.'

He turned and smiled, raised his glass to me. 'Don't make it hard for me, Harry. I just mean for a few minutes. I was so worried about you.'

I smiled at him again. 'That's nice.'

He eyed me warily over the rim of his glass and took two long gulps.

'So how are things?' I said brightly.

'I'll be honest with you, Harry,' he said. 'I wish . . .'

'Sssh.' I put a finger to his lips. I didn't want to hear it. Instead I looked full into his face. 'Robin,' I murmured, resting my hand on his leg. I felt his quadriceps twitch as though I had given him an electric shock. But when I glanced at his face he was still smiling. He was not really shocked. Instead, knowing I was throwing down the gauntlet, he was enjoying himself.

So was I. My vulnerability was working as an aphrodisiac on him.

I felt him harden against me. 'Harry, I don't want a divorce. Please, let me come home.'

But I was more powerful than I had been eleven months ago, more powerful and more cruel. I was tempted to mock him. I even thought of the right phrase. *Not down on your knees, Robin?* It stuck in my throat.

'I want to come back.' The sincerity in his voice was more of the same deceitful seduction. 'I miss you and Rosie.' He grinned. 'I'm actually quite lonely.'

'What about . . .?'

Now it was he who shushed me with a finger pressed to the lips. 'Don't even mention her.'

I was happy to oblige, for now.

'All I can say is it isn't any good. And it never will be.'

I should have felt elated to have had so much handed back to me. I didn't. His offer felt like something from old charity shops, the soiled, worn goods, so much less attractive or valuable than when new. I felt incredibly flat and

Robin must have sensed it. His jaw tightened and I knew he would not plead again. It was now or never.

I stood up, agitated. 'I need time,' I said, 'to think.'

Robin stood up too. 'How long, Harry?' It was the humblest I had ever heard from him.

'I'll tell you what,' I said. 'I promise I will let you know on New Year's Eve.'

He gave me a strange look. 'That's weeks away.'

'I know,' I said. 'But it seems fitting because that was when this whole, sorry business started.' I remembered then that I had never confided my Yuletide superstitions to him as he had never confided his fears to me.

'Robin,' I said, 'Who is Lorna Garbett?'

'How on earth did you . . .?'

'You left a little shoe box.'

He laughed. 'My old treasures.'

'A funeral notice?'

His face took on a bleak expression. 'She was my grand-mother,' he said finally. 'Mother's mother. She died of cancer when I was six years old. Mother took me to see her, lying in an open coffin. For weeks it gave me nightmares. I thought she would haunt me. She was like a living skeleton when she died. Bones sticking out.'

'But you kept the funeral announcement.'

His clear blue eyes met mine. 'Believe it or not I was fond of the old dear.'

I was silent.

'So New Year's Eve?'

Now I knew why our marriage had failed. Before I had cared too much, let him know I worshipped him, adored him. As the seducer playing a part I would be much more successful. I was in control now. Not Robin. I curled my arm back around his neck, dropped us both back on the sofa and played my part.

Chapter Sixteen

PC Harper was waiting for me at eleven o'clock the next morning ready to take my statement, ponderously writing longhand. The slow, deliberate action robbed the entire event of drama. I kept butting in, trying to make him put the right emotions into the words.

'He held a knife against me.'

'A weapon was used.'

'It tore my coat.'

'Damaging the victim's underwear.'

'I was frightened.'

He met my eyes briefly. There was no sympathy. Instead he pushed the pages towards me. 'Is that correct?'

I nodded.

'There is another thing,' he said and dropped a large album onto the desk.

'This is our "rogues' gallery".' He was making an attempt to be funny and friendly. No mention today of the Temgesic. He and I were on the same side now. *This was illusion. He knew something I did not.*

Even as I picked out Danny Small almost too easily I felt betrayed. Harper should have felt more of an ally. Instead there was a careful distance between us.

I jabbed my finger on the centre of his face, right over the nostril. The mug shot had all the details, the thin, rather ratty face, hair shaven short, gold sleeper in one ear, small, frightened eyes, an indecisive mouth.

'What will you charge him with?' I asked curiously.

'Aggravated robbery,' he said, 'for a start. We might have a go at ABH. He did assault you with a knife.' He clipped the sheaf of papers together. 'We could even have a go at possession. The Temgesic,' he explained nicely. 'If there had been a few more we might have tagged on

170

"With Intent to Supply" but with so few tablets it wouldn't stick.' He had rather nice green eyes, even if they did bulge, a big head and a lovely, ugly smile which I did not quite trust.

'And will he go to prison?'

Now he was perceptibly embarrassed. 'It's difficult to say at this stage, Doctor.'

My hands locked together beneath the desk. 'But it was a violent crime. And he threatened my daughter.' Even as I spoke I realised what a fool I must sound. To the police this was a minor assault. They must be used to worse things than this, rape, assaults which left their victims on life support machines. Murder.

'Uum, how long have you worked in this station?'

He was unsuspicious. 'Nearly fifteen years.'

'Then you must remember other cases.'

He nodded sagely.

'Like the little girl who went missing. What was her name now? Melanie.'

'I do,' he said. 'My first serious case.'

I leaned half across the desk. 'And you charged no one?'

'We never even found the body.'

'You had no one under suspicion?'

'We had our ideas.'

Harper was an innocent. And I wanted him to talk.

'I know the family.'

'I thought they were from London.'

'They were,' I said. 'I mean the grandparents. Her grandfather was a patient of mine.'

The green eyes fixed on mine. Maybe Harper wasn't so slow.

I needed to prompt him. 'He died recently, still under a shadow.'

'I never thought he had anything to do with it,' Harper said slowly, ponderously.

'So who?'

But he hid behind his woodenness. 'We had our suspicions.'

It was Pritchard. I could sense that slimy presence. They had suspected him, questioned him. Known it was him and been forced to let him go.

'There have been no more murders here,' Harper said stiffly.

But I knew there had. One many years ago. Somehow either Anthony Pritchard or his mother had poisoned Rupert Pritchard. And they had got away with it except for the old woman's conscience that made her death-bed confession inevitable. And if Pritchard had successfully murdered his father what about his mother? How had she died? Of the same substance?

I had arranged to meet Jay Gordon in the bar of the Silken Thread, a small pub of the Victorian era that the major brewers had yet to get their hands on and make soulless. I arrived first and bought a glass of wine, sat in the corner and waited. He turned up ten minutes late, full of apologies but neatly dressed in dark jeans and a sombre sweater.

He grinned his hello together with an apology. 'I'm sorry,' he said. 'The boys just didn't want to settle. And the more I tried to hurry them the more they delayed me. Let me get you a drink.'

It didn't matter. I had used the time to plan. It was no use being too blunt about this. I could make Jay Gordon my ally. At the school he could be my eyes and ears, protect the children, protect Rosie. For that I needed to take him into my confidence. It did not occur to me that he might take the same attitude that Arthur had, namely that having been neither formally charged nor found guilty Pritchard was innocent.

Could no one see it clearly as I did?

As soon as he was sitting opposite me I took the cue, mentioning his sons had helped me. 'How old are your boys?'

'Seven and nine.'

'You're divorced?' He nodded.

'But the boys didn't go with their mother?'

'She wasn't fit,' he said and I dropped the subject.

'You must find it hard.'

'No worse than thousands of other single parent families.'

I steered the conversation round. 'Being responsible for two children.'

I could see deep in his eyes he was puzzled by the direction of our conversation. He knew I wanted something from him but didn't have a clue what.

'And are they in Merrivale Primary?'

Again his nod held that vaguely puzzled look.

I admit I found him pleasant, intelligent company. His face was inoffensive and Rosie liked him. But that was not my reason for meeting him at all. I needed someone on my side, someone at the school. Pritchard must be watched. Who better than a teacher?

I plunged in. 'Did you know that your janitor was once held on a charge of suspected child abduction?'

It was too soon. I could feel alienation like a chilling breeze. 'I had heard a rumour,' he said carefully.

I stood up quickly. 'Let me get you another drink.' It had been too obvious. There was something faintly regretful in his smile now, as though he had thought he would find me congenial company. And I had disappointed him. I knew it when I handed him a full pint beer glass.

'You know Pritchard wasn't found guilty,' he said awkwardly. 'It really isn't fair for you to judge him. The police would have acted if . . .' His fine eyes held mine. 'If you know something definite, Harriet, you should pass it on. Otherwise . . .'

'I have a daughter,' I said. 'She's nine years old. Melanie Carnforth was just six when she vanished. She has never been seen since.'

'Pritchard's fond of children,' he protested. 'It's nothing unhealthy. He just likes them. That's all.'

I was quick. 'Are you so sure? Would you let your sons go out alone with him?'

Jay Gordon drained his glass and I knew I'd blown it. 'I'm sorry, Harriet,' he said. 'I promised the babysitter I wouldn't go out for long. And I've got exam papers to mark.'

As a double excuse it was pathetic. I froze out a smile. 'Fine,' I said. 'See you around.' It was a phrase I'd picked out from one of the soaps. It sounded just as false coming from my lips.

That was it. A wasted chance. And that hurt just as much as the telephone call from the police to say no charges would be brought in connection with the incident of last week.

Danny Small, it seemed, had an alibi.

Chapter Seventeen

Another tired night on call. Another bleep. Another message. Another plea for help.

And this time it was from Danny Small.

I could have left it. I would have been perfectly justified. We don't have to go to violent patients. We have a choice. We can divert them to the local casualty or we can opt for a police escort. I chose the police escort because I *wanted* to go.

Don't question why.

I checked my battered bag for equipment. It was complete. The nurse had restocked it with missing drugs. I waited outside my front door for the constable to arrive.

Not PC Harper this time but a burly young thing of less than twenty who answered to the name of Wagstaff. PC Wagstaff. I never did know his Christian name. He was as tall as a tree with long, dangling arms.

And he looked dubious. 'You're sure you want to go on this? I know you've had some trouble.'

'Absolutely sure. I'm a doctor, Police Constable Wagstaff. I have a duty of care.'

He still looked unhappy. 'You could just call an ambulance,' he said.

'Oh no. I want to go. You see, I know Danny.'

The words would be used later against me. *'The doctor said she wanted to go.'* And he would add, *'Yes, I did think it strange, especially under the circumstances.'*

Wagstaff still looked unhappy as though he sensed something was not quite right.

'Do you want to come in the squad car, Doctor?'

'Oh no,' I said. 'I'll drive myself. You follow.'

I caught him looking at me with a troubled expression as I switched my engine on.

Danny lived in a hostel, a well-known place to both myself and PC Wagstaff, a narrow, terraced house in a backstreet of Larkdale. All the occupants had their rents paid by the Social Services, their drugs supplied by Substance Abuse. They had virtually all they needed. Drugs, fags, money, food. In that order. But it was never quite enough.

The door was tugged open by a girl with wild, dry hair. She saw the police uniform and made a face. 'Yeah?'

I stepped from behind Wagstaff to take control. 'I'm the doctor,' I said crisply. Pale eyes widened. Like the magic words, Open Sesame, the door swung open.

'Tell me what's happened?'

'I dunno,' she said with a swift glance back at the uniform.

I kept my voice low. 'My only chance of doing any good is if I know the truth. What's he taken?'

Something very like fear licked her eyes and without another word she led the way up the dark stairs filled with sweet, sickly air. PC Wagstaff sniffed stagily. 'Nice air freshener, love.'

She stopped right there, halfway up the claustrophobic staircase. 'Thanks,' she said. 'It's called Opium.'

Give Wagstaff his due, his feathers were perfectly unruffled. 'I thought it was,' he said, and we finished our journey two flights up in the attic room by which time I had worked it out. This was probably the bitch who had given Danny his fake alibi and robbed me of a rightful conviction.

I said nothing but I noticed she made no attempt to enter the garret but hung back in the doorway as Wagstaff and I entered.

Vomit not only has different sounds but it has different smells to the practised nose. Danny had been vomiting bile over the one object in the room, a heap of blankets. This was where Danny lived, in this dingy rathole. I used my torch. One quick look at fixed, dilated pupils and I knew for once in his brief life Danny had had enough. Correction. This time Danny had had too much. I shouted in his ear, jabbed a needle into his skin to test his consciousness level. He didn't even feel that. He was far away. I looked up at the girl for explanation.

'He got it from the doctor's bag,' she said sulkily. 'He got the pure this time.' I could have sworn there was a note of envy in her voice.

'You bloody idiot,' I said. 'You lot never learn, do you? The stuff you get on the streets is something like twenty per cent – if that. He's OD'd.' From my bag I drew up the Narcan, instructed Wagstaff to squeeze Danny's arm, found a vein and shot it full of the antidote to his sad little habit. Wagstaff used his radio to summon an ambulance and we heard it tracking down the High Street. Danny was no longer my problem. In fact I didn't even wait for them to manhandle him down the stairs and into the van but went straight home.

I had had enough drama for one day.

On that Saturday Duncan rang me. 'You said you were interested in fungi,' he said. 'I noticed a lovely fairy ring in the field near the Heron Pool. Why don't you and Rosie come for a walk? I can point some of them out. It's a good time of year. Most fungi are at their best. A couple of weeks, Harry, first frosts and they'll all be gone.'

I was glad of the invitation. Rosie had been significantly quieter since Robin's brief forage back into family life. I'd heard nothing since. Not even the traditional bunch of red roses. I would have liked some red roses. Surely I had earned them. But nothing, and I knew that Robin, with acute perception, had sussed me out. He knew I had finally risen above my involvement with him. I was cast free. Maybe his ego had finally been dented. Who knew? Without contact I had no idea. For me I did not care. But for Rosie I was furious. Now love and involvement had finally withered and died I could even dislike him for his neglect of his own flesh and blood.

Of course there was always one explanation I could cling on to. Perhaps, just perhaps, he had decided to make no attempt to influence my decision. Of all the explanations it was the one I liked most.

So Duncan's chatter was doubly welcome. 'And besides the champignon, there was a lovely patch of *Amanita virosa* not far from the Heron Pool, you know. You might even have noticed it.'

'Sorry?' The name was foreign to me, foreign and yet familiar.

'*Amanita virosa,*' he said. 'The second deadliest fungus growing in the British Isles. A fry-up with some of these would probably kill you or at least give you stomach cramp, vomiting. You know. Pretty typical symptoms. They call it the Destroying Angel.'

Chapter Eighteen

Sometimes it takes a few days for bad news to filter through to us so that weekend I was ignorant. I had assumed that Danny would be admitted, the antidote already taking effect. He would be healed and counselled and the round of the Substance Abuse Unit, methadone supply and petty crime would continue. I did not know that, like Amelia Pritchard, he too had dropped out of the dance.

I was unsuspicious as I drove towards the Heron Pool, anticipating a brisk walk through the wood on a bright, autumn morning. But even this innocent forage would assume significance.

Duncan had been waiting for us, already leaning against the stone parapet as I had pulled the car into the field entrance, hoping I wouldn't get stuck. The mud looked soft. Rosie leapt out of the car, as energetic as a puppy. And I noticed that she hugged Duncan and greeted him with uncharacteristic familiarity, linking her arm through his.

'Hello there,' she said. 'I hope you're going to show us some really poisonous funguses.'

I winced. I'd been telling her all last night that the plural of fungus was not funguses.

Duncan corrected her gently and she laughed. 'I know what Mummy told me,' she said, 'but I was thinking about it all last night and it jolly well ought to be funguses. So that's what I decided to call them.' She gazed at both of us in turn with a challenging look.

I suppressed my laugh because I admired this childishly logical yet confident statement. But underneath I was concerned. This was an unfamiliar Rosie and it struck me that maybe she wanted her father so much she welcomed any male approach. She hardly knew Duncan yet she was chattering easily to him.

He didn't seem to mind but took hold of Rosie's hand while we skirted the Heron Pool to find the path that cut through the trees. At first I was hardly listening as Duncan explained how a fungus obtains its nutrients from rotting vegetable matter. I was too busy absorbing the early morning scene to pay much attention to his slow, didactic words. The sun was barely up, casting a thin light across fields that steamed with chilly, early morning mist. And I was distracted by my thoughts. Apart from the fact that this was late autumn instead of hot summer this must have been how it was the morning that Melanie Carnforth disappeared. She too had vanished into the early morning mist. It would have been quiet here, like this morning, silent between the trees apart from birdsong, distant dogs barking, distant cars droning along the road. There would have been no one around. Except her killer. I peered through the trunks of trees, too close together for a clear view, mist deceiving me into imagining I could see something that couldn't be there.

They were yards ahead of me, he talking in the gruff, pedantic voice. And then I started listening to what he was saying.

'Fungi, Rosie,' he laughed again, 'or funguses if you want to be incorrect' – I thought it very neat: while acknowledging her right to pervert a word he was gently, and non-confrontationally, correcting her – 'obtain their food by digesting organic matter.'

'Animals, do you mean?' Rosie's clear voice piped up. But the phrases had whipped up the vision. A fairy ring growing above the dead body, rotting animal matter. A fungus that fed on the body of the dead child.

With the instinct of a whippet Duncan must have sensed something strange in me. He glanced back. 'You all right there, Harry? Not going too fast for you, are we?'

And Rosie's merry rejoinder. 'Oh come on, Mum.'

I watched them hand in hand as though they were part of that vision. I must keep up.

I had dressed Rosie in blue jeans and her scarlet anorak. I had a sudden, vivid vision of the woman she would one day become. It was strange. Robin was blessed with attractive, regular features, I with irregular ones. Rosie looked like neither of us yet sometimes Robin would flit across her face as though his shadow fell there. I knew I would love the woman she would become, the woman Melanie Carnforth had never had the chance to be. So I watched my daughter as though I was her shepherd as she and Duncan scrambled through the trees, peering into heaps of leaves, running and shouting as though they were both children. And Duncan called out the names, Latin and colloquial. They were such wonderful names. Death Cap. Blusher. Fly Agaric. Toadstool.

'Don't lick your fingers,' he warned as she bent to touch something and I caught up and peered over his shoulder at a white, mushroom-like fungus on a spindly stem.

'This is it,' he said triumphantly. 'The Destroying Angel, *Amanita virosa.*'

But I saw more than the slim, white, mushroom shapes. Broken stalks. Some had been harvested. Pritchard.

The scribbled words I had interpreted as being a woman's name, *Anita,* had been a clever diagnosis from a country doctor. He had known as I knew that Rupert Pritchard had died after eating these. Whether picked by his wife or his son, the dish had been prepared deliberately. And Amelia Pritchard? I would stake my reputation that she had died from the exact same cause. Either a suicide or a murder.

'Duncan,' I said softly. 'What happens if you' – the thought struck me like a hammer: *she* had not come out here to pick them because she was incapable. They had been picked for her – 'are fed these?'

'Whew.' He whistled through his teeth. 'The usual. Nausea, vomiting, abdominal pain, hallucinations, death.' He glanced at Rosie. She was listening hard. 'Not pleasant,' he said, 'so don't touch.'

181

Rosie squeaked. 'Oh, horrible things,' she said and swung her wellie towards them.

'No.' Duncan stopped her 'No. They have as much right as we to this earth. As much right as a bee or a wasp or even an adder.' His eyes were fixed on me. 'As much right as Danny Small.'

'What's a Danny Small?'

He was still watching me. 'A rather sad person,' he said and I felt uncomfortable. This was a coded message for something but I did not know what.

My mind was still too full of the Destroying Angel to give the matter much attention. I thought I knew it all. The devil spawned its own young. His father had been violent. Mother and son had stayed silent, stuck together in their crime. Amelia Pritchard had kept her mouth shut about her husband's death for nearly fifty years. No great struggle then to keep mum about an unknown child for only ten. She would have stuck by her son with the same dogged, blind loyalty that had prevented her from telling me the truth the night she had fallen. Knowing her son was guilty she had still shielded him – again.

'Harriet,' Duncan and Rosie were waiting for me. We moved on, climbing over fallen, rotting tree stumps, finding Orange Peel and Witches' Butter, a huge Beefsteak Fungus just like the one that grew on the rotting tree stump which marked the spot where Melanie Carnforth had climbed over the fence.

'Look here. What a find.' Duncan's voice penetrated with the quick words of an enthusiast. 'Fly agaric.' He and Rosie knelt in the damp leaves to take a closer look.

I too peered at the red and white spotted fungus but it was another, more disturbing vision that formed in my mind. It was not clear, very fuzzy in parts but the main ingredients were there, almost visible. The child in the fly agaric dress, the man who held her hand and promised to show her fairy rings and toad-stools. The child would instinctively have trusted such a man. She would have gone with him, slipping her hand into his, as was Rosie now.

Melanie Carnforth had never seemed so close.

Reuben's voice whispered hoarsely in my ear. 'Help me, Doctor. Help me.' He had wanted me to find both her body and her killer.

I ran after them. 'Don't go so fast. Wait for me. Please?'

Rosie turned, irritated and I knew she was comfortable with Duncan. But I was beginning to understand things.

Instinct, superstition, call it what you like.

I knew.

He had held her by the hand, pretending to be her friend.

The vision stayed clear right through the walk and the lunch later with Fiona and Merryn. In fact it stayed with me for the whole weekend. By Monday I felt I would burst unless I spoke to someone about it. And Neil seemed ideal.

I found him in his surgery well before our first patients had arrived. But his eyes were very hostile as I blurted out the garbled story, knowing that to him it must have sounded worse than muddled, crazy. Toad-stools and poisonings, a murdered child whose body the entire Lark-dale police force had been unable to find. And here was I telling him not only that I knew how the child had been tempted beyond the boundary her grandparents had set but that the spot was marked by a fairy ring.

He frowned at me. 'What on earth are you saying?'

I cast around for something tangible to bear me out. 'I sent Amelia Pritchard's vomit away for analysis.'

'Not about that, Harriet,' he said impatiently. 'The little girl who vanished. How the hell do you know what happened?'

'I just know it, Neil.'

'So why didn't the police locate the body? They must have searched the forest thoroughly. It's the obvious place.'

'I don't know,' I said.

183

'Hmm.' He looked unimpressed. 'It beats me Harry, why you're so obsessed with something that happened so long ago.'

'Reuben asked me to help him.'

Neil looked cross. 'You don't think he might have been asking you to help in a terminal illness? For goodness' sake, Harriet. You were his doctor. Not a detective. If you know something tell the police. If not shut up before you find yourself in front of the courts as well as the General Medical Council. I can't understand you taking such risks. It's vastly unprofessional. Duncan and I will be very unhappy if you pursue this matter – for whatever reason.'

'But they never caught him.'

'Oh.' His face cleared. 'So you're still certain it was Pritchard?'

I nodded. 'And now he's got a job at the school.'

'Speak to the headmaster then.'

'I did.' I recalled the headmaster's look of hostility as I had related my observations. Worse, I remembered Jay Gordon's expression of dislike. In Larkdale, it seemed, the citizens preferred to forget than to know.

'And what do you propose doing about all this?' Neil's eyes were already wandering towards the buzzer and his overflowing basket of notes.

I stood up. 'I'm not going to rest, Neil. The man is a danger.' I felt my voice match his face with hostility. 'Don't you read your papers, Neil? Paedophiles are never to be trusted again. Not ever. They are never safe.'

His eyes dropped. He had the manners not to let me read the alienation he was feeling. 'Even ten years later? And he's clean.'

'What about his mother? She would have known, you see.'

'Harriet,' he said wearily, 'you have no proof. The woman almost certainly died of acute gastroenteritis. And if what you told me about the filth around that place is true

184

I'm really surprised she survived for so long without getting gut rot.'

'I shall prove that first,' I said, 'before I make it my business to clear Reuben Carnforth's name and find the body of that poor child so Vera can eventually be at peace.'

Neil looked almost sorry for me. 'Harry,' he said, 'it's been a shocking year for you, Robin and all that.' He looked embarrassed. 'Now don't take this the wrong way but you need a rest.'

The worst thing was I could read his mind. He had all but told me I was having a nervous breakdown, or to put it in neater, medical terms, acute anxiety and depression leading to psychosis.

He thought I was mad.

I left the room knowing that whereas Neil and I might have been friends, now we were uneasy partners. I thought I had reached rock bottom in his estimation. I had further to fall.

The last thing I needed was to have Fern on the phone to say that Anthony Pritchard had shown up at the surgery and was demanding to speak to me.

I was tempted to make him wait until the end but even knowing he was in the building was enough to disturb me. I could no longer concentrate. Feeling defeated I picked up the telephone. 'OK,' I said. 'You'll have to send him in.'

This time I did hear his footsteps approach. Pritchard was angry. Not tentative now. His knock was a loud rap. And he walked in without waiting for me to call him in.

But I had noticed I felt none of my usual apprehension or discomfort. Rather I welcomed a confrontation. I wanted to see his face when I told him I knew the police had been wrong to release him. I wanted to tell him I knew he had murdered Melanie, that I knew why too. I thought things would soon be out in the open, not hidden any more.

Thank goodness I didn't.

His face was pale and he was sweating. 'I want to know what's going on.'

'What do you mean, Mr Pritchard?'

'They aren't allowing me to bury my mother. They say that you won't authorise it.'

'Mr Pritchard,' I said steadily, 'it isn't up to me but the coroner. I can't give a cause of death so am unable to fill in the death certificate. No one knows what your mother died of.'

He was breathing quickly. 'You attended her not long before she died. She was an old lady in poor health. Isn't that enough?'

'No,' I said. 'It isn't. I attended your mother for a simple injury. There was nothing there that would have killed her.' I was sure he was hiding something.

'My mother,' he said, 'Was eighty-four years old. I don't know why people have to be so curious about what exactly she died of that they have to hack open an old woman.'

'It is normal practice, Mr Pritchard, for any death that occurs within twenty-four hours of hospital admission to be brought to the attention of the coroner.'

I had forgotten Pritchard was clever. 'Brought to the attention,' he said, staring at me. 'That doesn't always mean they have to have a post mortem.'

His eyes were magnified behind the hyperopic glasses. His breath was on me, musty and old. I felt I was back in that stuffy claustrophobic bedroom, the faint smell of urine, the chill, the unopened windows, the Chinese coolie lampshade, swinging. 'Why couldn't you leave well alone?' he said, with a venomous look. 'It was all your fault. Why did you have to dig, ask questions, disturb old people? My mother and I had come to terms with things. We'd worked our lives out. Then you start by asking about my father. I knew it was upsetting mother when I said you'd asked. It made her nervous. She wasn't herself after that.'

I couldn't help myself. 'And Melanie Carnforth?'

Pritchard went pale. 'You surely can't be thinking of dragging that all up too?' A spasm of pain crossed his face. 'Even the police had to admit I had nothing to do with that poor little girl. What's it got to do with you, all these things? You're a doctor. More than that you're *my* doctor. You're supposed to look after *me*. You have no right to make these accusations. Oh.' He dropped his face into his hands. 'What do I have to do to convince you I had nothing to do with that poor child going missing? It was nothing to do with me. I didn't know anything about it.'

I was silent. It suddenly hit me that I had overshot the mark. If Pritchard had made a formal complaint he would find a ready ear in the Medical Defence Union, the health authority, my partners . . . Neil's face flashed across my eyes. He already had his doubts about the balance of my mind.

I held my breath.

But Pritchard had no real fight in him. He shuffled out of the room. Defeated. Or so I thought. I never saw a man look so guilty. Or so I thought.

At the time my mind was still on the results of the tests on Amelia's stomach contents. I knew they would contain traces of the muscarinic agent found in *Amanita virosa,* the Destroying Angel. Later, I thought, I would ring the lab in Birmingham. I didn't get the chance.

As soon as I had finished surgery they were waiting for me. Not PC Harper or the pleasant PC Wagstaff. This was a plain clothes detective with small, darting eyes that seemed to absorb everything in my surgery only to distort it. Sharply she introduced herself as Detective Inspector Angela Skilton before commenting on the state of my walls.

'Someone threw my plant pot at it.' I was nervously wondering why she had come here. And I didn't like the fact that she wasn't coming straight to the point. 'I'm having the room redecorated next week while my partner is on holiday,' I added, wondering what it had to do with her anyway.

'I'm here about one of your patients,' she said in her sharply acid voice. 'Danny Small.'

'I saw him last week,' I said. 'Drugs overdose. How is he?'

'Dead.'

'But . . .'

'He died of an overdose of diamorphine.'

I shook my head. 'I thought the Narcan would have pulled him out of it.'

DI Skilton took some time consulting her notes before looking back at me. 'Would you mind explaining to me exactly what Narcan is?'

I swallowed my surprise. I had a bad feeling about this one. 'I diagnosed Danny as suffering from an overdose of opiates,' I explained. 'Narcan is the antidote. It's as simple as that. He was comatosed when I got there but the Narcan should have pulled him out of the coma. Reversed the effects?' I wasn't convinced I was getting through to her.

'I see.' She wasn't writing anything down. Instead she was eyeing me gravely. 'And you gave him . . .?'

'A therapeutic dose of Narcan,' I said patiently.

'Doctor . . .' The clever eyes were fixed on mine. 'Did you form any conclusion about the diamorphine?'

'Sorry?'

'PC Wagstaff,' now she was consulting the notebook, 'overheard you make some comment about the drug.'

The fug in my brain cleared then. 'Yes,' I said. 'The girl living there told me Danny had pilfered another doctor's bag.'

'I see.'

'Do you know anything more about where Danny got the diamorphine from?'

'No.'

188

Clever DI Skilton was shaking her head. 'As you probably know, Doctor, the diamorphine supplied to doctors is
pure,' she said. 'It's pure and white.' There was some point
to her telling me this but I couldn't yet work out what it was.
'The stuff the dealers peddle on the streets is rough, comes
from the fields of Central America, some from other countries. Afghanistan for instance. It's brown.' She licked her
lips. 'By the time the dealers have cut it it's usually about
twenty per cent pure – if that.'

'I know all this,' I said irritably.

'The trouble is, Doctor, when the addicts get hold of the
real, one hundred per cent stuff, they invariably overdose
on it.' She paused. 'There is a death almost every time.'

And this time it was Danny.' I was stating the obvious.

'Quite,' she said. 'I understand you had been having a
bit of trouble with him.'

'Yes,' I said uneasily, 'but we were going to remove
him from our list. He wasn't a problem.' I could not
understand why I was so anxious to take this stance.
Danny was a problem. He had angered me, frightened
me, threatened me, robbed me. Of course he was a
bloody problem.

She was equal to this. 'I understand removal from a
doctors' list normally takes about three weeks.' Precise and
hostile, she was checking her facts as she went along.

'Not if there's violence involved, which of course there
was.'

'In which case?'

'Immediately.'

She leaned forward. 'So why did you go out to him that
night?'

I licked my lips. I could see how this was looking.

'Why didn't you just call an ambulance?'

'I. . . I. . .' I found it impossible to explain. To tell this
hard-nosed woman that I was a doctor and therefore owed
Danny a duty of care would not convince her. Besides, it

189

wasn't the truth. I had relished the feeling of power of life or death over him.

Her eyes were on me as she asked her next question. 'Did you dislike the deceased?'

It took a bit of adjustment thinking of Danny as 'the deceased'. I shook my head. 'No,' I said. 'I did not dislike the deceased. But I resented the time wasted dealing with drug addicts. We are trained to deal with genuine sickness. Not self-abuse.'

But I knew these were transparent lies. I *had* disliked Danny. In fact I had hated him. For threatening Rosie I had hated him. And as I had stood over him, unconscious, breathing noisy and deep, I had experienced a brief, gloating moment of power.

I had looked at the barrel of the syringe and gloated in the knowledge that if I gave him the contents IV he would live. If not he would die. This was more just than the law itself, better than a weak jury, a benevolent, misguided judge. It had put the power into the hands of the victim, me.

Skilton was watching me with eyes as piercing as an owl's. 'Tell me, doctor,' she said. 'How exactly does this drug . . .'

'Narcan.'

'How is it packaged?'

'It comes in a glass phial with a rubber bung.'

'Do you still have the phial?'

'No, I don't.'

'So what happens to them?'

'I put them with the syringe and needles into . . .' And I remembered the yellow plastic sharps box sitting on the passenger seat of my car. 'My Lego Box', Rosie called it.

Skilton was reading my mind. 'You discard them in a special container?'

She already knew. The bitch had known before she had come into the surgery. I realised then that I was in trouble. 'The one on the passenger seat of your car?'

190

I nodded.

So did she. Then she held out her hand for the car keys. 'Would you mind?'

I gave them to her

'There's another point I'd like to clarify with you,' she said. 'You say the diamorphine came from a doctor's bag?'

I was perhaps a little too eager to supply the information. 'His girlfriend told me,' I said quickly. 'They had robbed another doctor's bag.'

Skilton shook her head. 'Only yours, Dr Lamont. There has been no other report of a doctor's bag being stolen. And in your report you mentioned no diamorphine.'

I felt my neck grow hot. 'There wasn't any. I don't think any of us keep that sort of stuff in our bags. It wouldn't be justified.'

I could see the suspicion grow in her face as well as hear it in her voice. 'Well, as I said, we have no reports of doctors' bags going missing – except yours.' She was threateningly quiet for a minute or two before adding, 'And then there's this business of the Narcan you claim to have given.'

'I beg your pardon?'

'At post mortem they biopsied the tissue around your injection site.'

I was angry at this professional snooping. 'Why?'

'Because the physician who admitted Danny made the comment that he was surprised the GP had failed to administer the antidote.' She was reading from her notes again. Every time her head dropped it had implications. 'Look, doctor.' Her tone was pseudo-conciliatory. 'I'm no expert. I'm just a detective. I don't know anything about any of the drugs except the ones that get flogged on street corners.' She smiled and I realised that had been an attempt at a joke. 'I'm just here to ask a few questions and try to clarify matters. Firstly. Did you have diamorphine in your doctor's bag on the night that Danny Small threatened and robbed you?'

'No.'

'Secondly. Did you give the antidote to Danny when you realised that he was suffering from an overdose of diamorphine?'

'Yes. I did,' I said. 'Whatever the post mortem findings are I gave him an intravenous injection of Narcan. Police Constable Wagstaff saw me. It should have saved his life.'

'Thank you, Doctor,' she said. She gave a tight-lipped smile. 'There is just one other point I'd like to clear up.' No need for her to read this from her pad. She knew this bit off by heart. 'He'd made threats against your daughter.' Her smile this time was bordering on chummy. 'I've got a daughter, Dr Lamont. I'd hate anyone who threatened my daughter.'

I wasn't going to fall into that trap. 'I didn't take the threats seriously,' I said.

'Ah,' she said slowly, 'but the investigating officer says you did. He said you seemed quite upset by them. So it must have been terrible for you to realise that we wouldn't be pressing any charges.'

With the best imagination in the world she could never know how terrible.

Chapter Nineteen

I had only one consolation in the dying days of November and early days of December. Ruth burst into surgery late one Thursday evening, her bump proudly prominent. She sat opposite me. 'Wonderful to see you, Harry,' she said. 'And how are things?'

'Complicated,' I said guardedly. 'Very complicated.'

Thankfully she didn't seem to know anything about Danny Small's death.

'Did you do anything about Pritchard?'

I shook my head. 'I did but I didn't get anywhere. The headmaster thinks I'm gunning for him. The police consider the Melanie Carnforth case closed. Even Neil seems to think I'm going a bit over the top. No one believes there's any cause for concern. They think he's safe now.'

'Well, I don't,' she said firmly. 'And the trouble with situations like this is that no one takes a blind bit of notice until something happens again.' Her face was earnest. 'Maybe if they'd found the child's body in the first place there would have been something to connect him. But I suppose without that . . .' She looked troubled. 'You have to do something.'

'But until Pritchard makes a move . . .'

Ruth nodded sagely. 'Then we'll get him, Harry,' she said, 'because we're both keeping an eye on him. We know.'

I measured Ruth's blood pressure and took her urine and blood samples before asking her to lie on the couch. Obediently she lay down and proffered her swollen belly. I put my hands on just above the umbilicus.

It was a miracle. I felt the baby kick. Not just kick. It kicked me.

I had felt babies kick before. But this was different. This was Ruth's child, conceived against all odds, in spite of my warnings.

She raised herself on her elbow and touched my wrist almost timidly. 'That's why we have to preserve the sanctity of life,' she said. She heaved her swollen abdomen upright. 'Life is too precious to have it wasted – ever in any way, for any reason.' Her face clouded. 'That poor child,' she said, pulling her dress down over her abdomen. Her thoughts had returned to Melanie. Maybe it was Ruth's sentiments that spurred me on but I knew it was time to talk to Vera.

There was snow in the air as I crossed the causeway early in December and turned right to climb the hill to the farm. The fields were iced with frost and there was not an animal in sight. Even they were sheltering. The cold conjured up a memory of Reuben. I recalled saying something to him one day about the freezing weather, almost apologising for the cold. He'd given me a puzzled look. His face had been still craggy then; it had been before the cancer had pared it to the bone. 'We farmers,' he had said, 'we welcome the frost. It's one of the times we can get a tractor on the field without getting bogged down.' And he'd chuckled at me, a townie, who didn't understand that to the farmers there was both good and bad in all weathers. And as I shivered I recalled that in the years that I had known him I had never heard him complain about anything. Not even that final, debilitating illness.

He had been a good man. I owed it to him to clear his name.

'Help me.'

I scanned the woods and saw nothing but dark trees, pressing together, shielding any view.

Vera was surprised to see me. 'Well, doctor,' she said, 'there's no one ill here today.' But the wide smile on her face robbed the words of any sense of dismissal. Instead she held the door open and welcomed me in for some tea.

'Now what's brought you up here?' she asked. 'And don't try telling me you were just passing.'

I laughed, feeling more at home here than I had done for the entire year. I felt as though now I could be honest with her.

'I came to talk to you about Melanie,' I said.

Apart from a slight raising of the eyebrows I wouldn't have been certain that Vera had even heard. When she did finally speak she sounded puzzled. 'But it happened such a long time ago, Doctor. You never even knew her. Why are you so interested?'

'Because Reuben wanted me to help,' I said simply.

She brushed my hand and repeated her earlier sentiments. 'He had such faith in you,' she said. 'Too much. I told him. But it's good of you to care.'

'I was fond of Reuben.'

'I know that,' she said. Then her face hardened. 'No one else cares in this town. To them our little girl was an outsider. Not one of theirs.'

'Maybe that's another reason why I feel involved.' I attempted a smile. 'I'm an outsider too. Or I feel one these days.'

'Mebbe,' she said.

'Vera,' I said tentatively. Even I hesitated to resurrect this particular ghost. I knew it was dangerous territory. 'Someone called Anthony Pritchard was questioned in connection with Melanie's disappearance?'

Puzzled, she nodded. 'Ye-es?'

'Did you think . . . ?'

She raised her head with great effort. 'I didn't know what to think,' she said. 'We all knew the Pritchards were strange folk. His mother kept herself to herself. His father died in peculiar circumstances.'

'I know all about that,' I said.

Her mouth puckered. 'You do?'

'Yes. What I want to know was, was there anything else that led the police to suspect Pritchard?'

'Well,' she thought for a minute. 'He lived near. I mean

195

not many people do live within a mile of this place. And Melanie can't have gone far.' Her eyes sparkled with tears. 'She was only six. And then there was the dress.'

'Where *exactly* did they find it?'

'Right at the top of Gordon's Lane,' she said quietly. 'Stuffed in the hedge.'

This was the most dangerous bit. 'Would it trouble you to know he's working with children, in a school?'

'I don't know,' she said wearily. 'I just don't know. I was never sure myself. I couldn't imagine him doing anything to her. He *seemed* harmless.' She fingered the sleeve of her sweater. 'You think it *was* him?'

I nodded and she stood up. 'Then I'm going to the police. I'm going to tell them. To think he's been sitting under our noses for all these years. I've spoken to him in the town. If I'd have known . . .' Hatred flashed across her face. 'I would have killed him myself.'

I shivered as a gust of icy wind found the gap beneath the door. 'Maybe you should wait until we've got proof before speaking to the police,' I said.

She sank back in the chair. 'I just want her found. As I've got older finding her seems the most important thing to me. I want her found even if it is just to lay her to rest with Reuben.'

'Do you?'

'Yes.'

'Then help me.'

Abruptly she left the room and when she came back she was holding something, a red, nylon rucksack, slightly worn and faded.

It was Melanie's.

'Her mother and father didn't want it,' she said. 'Neither did the police because she didn't have it with her that day. We kept it, Reuben and me. It was all we had left of her.' She slung it across her shoulders, far too small for an adult. But perfectly sized for a child of six. 'So proud of

196

it she was, when she arrived. Carrying all her own luggage. Like a big girl.'

Vera dropped the bag onto the table and I touched it superstitiously, as though I could divine the child's fate.

'You can borrow it,' she said, 'but I shall want it back.'

I picked it up and hugged it to me. 'Do you mind,' I said, 'if I walk across your field? There's something I want to look at.'

She gave a wry smile. 'Be my guest,' she said, 'but I shan't come with you. I've the cattle to feed before it gets dark.'

I said goodbye to her awkwardly, aware that by bringing up the subject I had reopened a painful wound, one that had healed over only lightly.

So I lifted the latch and crunched my way over the frosty field towards the line of trees until I reached the rotting stump. As I had suspected my dreams had not deceived me but had resurrected a subconscious visual image. The bracket fungus was the size of a saucer; brown and inches thick, just as it had been in my dream.

What else had I tucked away?

I stood for a while before mouthing a prayer of promise over Reuben's grave. Then I slung the tiny rucksack over my arm and walked back to my car. As I drove back down through the wood I kept glancing across at Melanie's bag. Mediums use articles to locate people, superstitiously believing they hold a latent force that will guide them.

Maybe this would lead me to the child. But I was passive about this belief, keeping it in my car for two whole days, picking it up whenever I could, even going so far as to bury my face in it. But no strange messages came from it, no electric impulses. Nothing. It simply lay there, an inanimate object. And inside were Melanie's clothes, shorts, T-shirts, spare trainers. No dresses. Like most girls she had spurned dresses – except the one.

It took two days of inactivity before I was spurred into action. I knew I must act *for* the child, firstly by chasing up the result of Amelia Pritchard's sample. That would be my angle of attack, reasoning. If I could put Pritchard under suspicion and thus back under the eyes of the police surely they would reconsider his involvement in Melanie's disappearance. And they might speak to the education authority and put a stop to him working at the school.

The lab was, as always, uncurious but factual. 'Some sort of muscarinic agent,' the technician reported.

'Can't you be a bit more specific?'

'Well, not really,' she said.

I tried to prompt her 'What are we talking about here? A drug?'

'Well, we can guess.'

'Go on.'

'Well,' she said, 'the trouble is that all the stomach contents had already been vomited up. That is, anything solid,' she finished apologetically. 'So all we've really got to work on are the toxins.'

This was cagey, defensive talk but I recognised it as the speech we all hide behind when we are not sure, having been trained not to make guesses. But it was no good to me. I needed facts.

'This woman died,' I said.

'I'm not surprised. The toxin level was very high.'

Again helpful but unhelpful. I had to show my hand. 'Could these toxic levels be due to ingestion of poisonous fungi?'

'Oh.' The chemist drew in a long breath. 'Well, maybe. I'd really have to know the circumstances a little better. It could be. Was the patient in the habit of getting up at dawn to harvest mushrooms?' It was a serious question but spoken in a jokey tone.

'No. She was more or less bedridden.'

'Well, I don't understand then how the mistake could have happened. I mean commercial growers . . .'

'It was no mistake.'

Silence down the phone. Then, 'Be very careful, Doctor.'

'Keep the sample,' I said, and put the phone down. I knew it now. Pritchard had fed his mother some of Duncan's favourite poisonous fungi. Maybe as a late revenge for his father's death. Maybe because Amelia knew something that made her a liability now I was showing an interest in Melanie's disappearance. Or was it the renewed interest in her late husband's death that had forced the issue out into the open? Perhaps she had started to ramble and the risk for Pritchard had been too great.

I picked the phone up again but this time I dialled the coroner's number. The official channels could deal with this aspect.

Give Lemming some credit. He listened. Right the way through before giving a long sigh. 'But Doctor, you say that your suspicions were aroused because the deceased's husband died almost fifty years ago in the same way?'

Even to my ears the entire hypothesis sounded weak. 'Ye-es.'

'Well,' he said reluctantly. 'I'll speak to the pathologist. I expect he'll have preserved some samples of his own.'

I risked all then. 'I think the fungus was *Amanita virosa*, the Destroying Angel.'

Lemming gave a sceptical 'Hmm. If there are any grounds for believing this' – he paused – 'fungus was ingested, I suppose I'll have to alert the police. I must say, Dr Lamont, your patients have an uncanny habit of dying in strange circumstances, don't they? I believe we have another police investigation concerning a second patient of yours? A drug addict?'

I could hardly reply, my mouth was suddenly dry. 'Yes.'

'Well, we've fixed the inquest for him early next week and I shall expect you to attend.'

And Mrs Pritchard?'

'Let's wait until we've got some toxicology reports, shall we, and see what the police turn up.'

Police? They surfaced the next morning. WDI Skilton looked as though she had been sucking lemons. Her mouth was puckered with disapproval. And she'd been lying in wait for me to finish my surgery. All bad signs.

'I'm afraid we have a slight problem,' she said in a polite voice.

I could play this game too. 'And what's that?' It seems funny to think I still felt no apprehension. I was still so sure that I had injected Narcan into Danny Small's battle-scarred little vein.

'Put it like this, Doctor. We found the ampoule of Narcan, as you suggested.'

I smiled smugly.

'And sent it away for analysis.'

The two of us were keeping the biochemist busy.

'But while it read Narcan on the label,' she said, 'the drug inside the glass phial,' she paused for full effect, 'was pure diamorphine.'

'What?' I was dazed. 'Are you saying someone switched drugs?' It made no sense.

'Exactly.' I could hear the dry rasp as she rubbed her hands together. 'You see, one of the technicians in the forensics laboratory was clever enough to examine the rubber bung in the top of the phial.'

I was still too dazed by the revelation to interpret what she obviously perceived as a significant fact.

'There were three holes in it, Doctor.' The sharp little eyes bored into mine with all the direction of a Black and Decker. 'Do you have any comment to make?'

I shook my head. There should only have been one, the one I would have made as I inserted a needle to extract the drug. Three meant . . . 'It doesn't make sense,' I managed.

She shook her head as though pitying me. 'No,' she said, 'it doesn't, not unless . . .'

Even I could work that one out. Someone had switched drugs. 'Fingerprints?' 'Yes,' she said. 'Yours.'

She let that sink right in before standing up. 'I have to inform you, Doctor,' she said, 'We're investigating this as a case of manslaughter. And to be perfectly frank with you we only have one suspect.'

'But I gave that injection in good faith, believing it to be Narcan.'

'We understand your claim that the drugs had been switched but look at it from our point of view, Dr Lamont. Who would want to switch the drugs around?'

I could think of no one. Certainly not Pritchard. Come to think of it, who had orchestrated my initial visit to Danny? Again I could think of no one.

I looked around my scarred room, my mind working the picture out in slow motion as though in a comic strip. Wagstaff had said there were three holes in the rubber bung when I knew I had only pushed the needle in once, into what I had assumed was a phial of a sterile and unused drug, straight from the manufacturer's. Three holes . . . The first to withdraw the Narcan. The second to insert the diamorphine. So mine would have been the third prick, made as I inserted the needle preparing to withdraw the drug ready to 'save' Danny Small's pathetic little life. Whatever my motive, what I had actually done had been to murder him because someone had switched drugs. But who had access to pure diamorphine? And I didn't just mean the stuff I had injected into Danny's arm but the original stuff he had overdosed on, the stuff supposedly sourced from *my* doctor's bag.

I knew I hadn't been carrying diamorphine when Danny had robbed me. Temgesic I might forget about. Diamorphine – not a chance.

You see we weren't talking about street dope here. We were talking about diamorphine of a sterile, surgical purity.

My suspicions were shifting. On top of the drug itself who would have had the medical knowledge to substitute an antidote for an agonist? Who on earth could have predicted or planned that Danny would collapse from an overdose on my night on call?

Wagstaff had spoken of a doctor's bag. I looked further. The hand that had held the phial had been wearing a surgical glove. We were talking about one of my colleagues.

What hope for you, Doctor, if your patients still have the power to manipulate you from beyond the grave?

Chapter Twenty

At the beginning of the year I had finally learned not to trust my husband. Now, as I sat in my scarred surgery, I decided that the same yardstick might apply to one of my partners. One of them had set me up to give Danny Small his last, lethal shot.

Which one?

The vision of Duncan, walking hand in hand with Rosie through the trees was a haunting one. But this was pure conjecture. On the surface Duncan seemed a happy family man, reluctant to see his daughter settle too far away. *On the surface.*

I tried to think whether I had ever seen Merryn with a boyfriend? No. It was an uncomfortable thought. I had believed I knew Duncan. Not as a child abuser, a killer, a man who would . . .

I stared through the window. What was I saying? That Danny had been killed purely to distract me from Melanie Carnforth's murder? Had I been getting too near? I shook my head, bemused. Apart from asking questions and pointing fingers I had found out *nothing* about Melanie's disappearance.

Had Danny been the real target, then? Why would anyone want to murder a crazed drug addict? Had *he* known something about the murder?

At the time when Melanie had disappeared he would have been a boy of around nine. Had he then, possibly, been a child who had wandered through the trees early on summer mornings? But if he had seen something why hadn't he told the police at the time? Why bottle it up only to use the knowledge manipulatively years later when the whole incident had been forgotten.

Except by me. Had I then resurrected an almost forgotten

image? Or had it been something he had found out more recently? And how would he use his knowledge?

The answer was daybright. To acquire drugs, of course. Danny would do anything to get drugs. The only thing I didn't know was what had been the knowledge? And who had he used it against?

There was another more uncomfortable thought. Had I been the true target? Had Danny Small been eliminated purely to discredit me, to prevent my questions about a dead child being heard?

And as I could suspect Duncan then Neil should share the umbrella of suspicion. Neil who hid everything from us apart from a choice, surface veneer. But at some point his wife had vanished, like Melanie Carnforth. And a year later his son too had gone. And we, his partners, had received no explanation. More incredible we had not asked for one but had politely allowed Neil to keep his secrets.

What secrets? Slowly I shook my head. Neil could not possibly have murdered Petra and concealed her death for a year. Sandy would have asked questions. So they had left and for a reason.

My hand wandered towards the telephone. I felt an overwhelming urge to share my suspicions. But who would I speak to? The police? They weren't interested in Melanie Carnforth's murder, only Danny Small's. And they had their chief suspect.

My hand slid back down to my lap. So it was up to me to investigate. But where should I start? Reluctantly I acknowledged that I had only one potential avenue of enquiry.

Danny Small's 'girlfriend'. And I didn't hold out much hope.

I muddled my way through my morning surgery and defaulted on the usual cup of coffee. I couldn't face sitting with Duncan and Neil, wondering over the rim of my mug which one it was who had killed Melanie Carnforth, only to follow up the crime ten years later. Because connection there was. Of that I was sure.

So instead I found my way to the terraced house again and stared up at the gable window which had marked Danny's room. I wondered who lived there now.

It only struck me that Danny's girlfriend might blame me for his death when her face appeared in an inch-wide crack in the door and she spoke with overt hostility.

'What do you want?'

'Please,' I said. 'Please, I want to ask you a few things.'

She opened the door just wide enough to snarl at me. 'Haven't you done enough? The police told me how Danny came to die. We came to you for help. And look what you done. You killed him.'

I jerked back. Theoretically she was right.

She tried to push the door closed but I heaved against it. 'I must explain.'

'Explain what? You bloody murdered him, you cow.'

'But . . .'

Her eyes were hot with hate. 'What is it with you doctors? You can't bloody well admit it when you've made a mistake, can you? You were wrong.'

'I gave him the wrong drug,' I said. 'But only because someone had switched the drug inside the phial.'

Her glare was even more hostile.

'Someone deliberately switched the drugs,' I insisted.

'Who then?' Her stare was challenging now. 'Who'd do such a thing? And why?'

My hands dropped to my side, uselessly.

She pushed her face out beyond the door. She believed she was calling my bluff. What she didn't understand was that it was the perfect cue.

'I think it was the same person who got him the stuff he OD'd on in the first place. Who was supplying him?'

'That was you,' she said, 'you cunt.' And she slammed the door in my face.

Three days later I was summoned to attend Danny Small's inquest. Inquests are informal affairs, held in coroners courts, a cross between a schoolroom and a court of law. Today's was poorly attended, by the police, the pathologist and a thin woman at the back in leggings and a balled blanket coat who sat huddled into the seat, as though to make herself invisible.

I caught sight of PC Wagstaff who struggled to avoid my eyes, and Detective Inspector Angela Skilton, who made no such effort but seemed to want to stare me out as though I would eventually collapse under the penetrating gaze of her hazel eyes. I sat, awkwardly, on the front row and waited to be called.

A coroner has a job; he has to ascertain who the deceased was, how, where and when they died. His is not the chore of pointing the finger but it was still up to me to tell my side of the story, clearly.

Lemming adjusted his gold-rimmed glasses. 'So you were summoned to the home of the deceased at?'

'Ten p.m.'

'Where?'

I supplied Danny's address.

'And what conclusion did you reach?'

'I decided that Danny Small was suffering from an over-dose of diamorphine.'

'What made you arrive at this diagnosis?'

'Personal history. He was comatosed with pin-point pupils and slow respirations.' I tried to moisten my lips. 'Although other diagnoses were possible I felt urgent action was required to prevent my patient's death.' I knew I had to justify my actions.

'So you decided to administer . . .?'

'Intravenous Narcan.'

He gave me an uncomfortable, stern look. 'And then what did you do, Doctor?'

'I drew a phial of Narcan from my bag.'

He interrupted me. 'The light, I assume, was poor?'

I knew what he was getting at. 'Not too poor for me to read the label on the phial.'

'And?'

'I injected 10 milligrams intravenously.'

The next look was more unfriendly. 'I have to say there appears to be a disparity between the findings of the pathologist and your evidence.'

So I had not imagined Lemming's hostility. It was real.

'I have no comment to make.' But I did. I wanted to defend myself. I wanted to make them all believe me.

Lemming sat on his high seat and shuffled his papers around before addressing the gathering. 'I have no option but to adjourn this inquest pending further forensic and police enquiries.'

The woman sat at the very back of the room burst into tears. She must be Danny's mother. It was a sobering thought.

I made my way back to the surgery feeling depressed and let myself in through the back door.

I spotted Duncan disappearing into his early evening surgery but although he must have seen me he pretended he hadn't. The action made me feel even more alone as I closed the door behind me and stared at my own four walls. But receptionists can be loyal beings. Fern Blacklay must have spotted me and immediately attacked me with paint cards. 'Choose your colour,' she said gaily.

Did she not know my very integrity as a doctor was under question, and with that not only my right to practise but potentially my right to freedom?

I tried to explain to her but she tossed her head.

'There's been some mistake, Doctor,' she said. 'Some awful mistake.'

I tried to pump her. Maybe she could put her finger on the guilty party. 'So how do you think I came to give the wrong drug?'

'They must have got muddled up.'

I tried again, none too subtly. 'You don't think one of the other doctors could *accidentally* have switched the drugs?'

'You can't go blaming one of your partners,' she said severely. 'The mistake won't have been theirs. I mean the stuff was in *your* bag.'

I persisted. 'You've never seen either of them touch my bag?'

Instantly she drew herself up to her full height, her eyes were hard. 'Certainly not. Doctor, what are you suggesting?'

I tried to say something but she put a hand on my shoulder. 'Look, Doctor,' she said. 'I know it isn't my place to say this. But I have known you for a number of years.'

I smiled weakly.

'Take a holiday,' she urged. 'You need a rest. It's been a stressful year for you. And the job isn't easy.'

Even the receptionists disbelieved me. I gave upthen, tried to repair some of the damage. 'So let's choose a colour.'

Fern must still have had some faith in me because she gave me a tentative smile. 'You'll feel better when Ferris has got rid of those horrible marks on your wall. You can move into Dr Anderson's room. He's away. Addicts,' she finished darkly. 'More trouble than they're worth.'

I jabbed my finger against a warm peach tone. I was still here, not Danny Small, not Amelia Pritchard. Not Neil.

'Did you say I was to move into Neil's room?'

She nodded. 'Ferris will have to get a move on. We've only got a week. It's now or never, Harriet.'

Now or never, I repeated. Now or never. I watched my eyes narrow in the mirror. Now.

So while the handyman wandered across the road to the DIY supermarket I moved my stuff into Neil's vacated room. Another holiday for him meant that he, at least, was out of the way. It would soon be Christmas. Cleverly, or so I thought, I reasoned that if I found evidence in Neil's room of his involvement with either Melanie or Danny, Duncan would be in the clear. But if I found nothing and believed that Neil was innocent then it *had* to be Duncan. Who else was there?

And for the first time because I linked the two crimes, I believed I could discount Pritchard. He had no access to doctors' supplies of diamorphine, Danny's original OD, the one that had lured me to his house in the first place. Neither would he have had the knowledge to switch a drug for its antidote.

Pritchard, I reasoned, was in the clear. Innocent of all but his mother's poisoning?

The questions were still tugging at my brain as I sat in the clinical whiteness of Neil's room and wondered. By the end of my morning surgery I was still wondering. The room was so bare, as though Neil had made an attempt to conceal the man he was. Unsurprisingly, unlike my room, there were no family photos. Petra and Sandy had vanished as if they had never been. *So where were they?*

I opened Neil's desk drawer. No. That is a lie. I did not simply open one drawer. I rifled through the entire room. I felt I must expose everything. Not just the poisons books and drugs bulletins, not just the medical journals and spare batteries for the auroscope. Not only the piles and piles of notes waiting for letters to be typed or reports to insurance companies. Everything.

I literally ransacked the room. There was nothing there. But then it was a very bare room, surgically sterile. Even the one picture was of a white mountain, sharp, pointed. No people. I picked it off the wall to read the title. The Andes.

But secrets can be found. And the back of this photograph could be removed – easily. Heaven knows why he had kept them there.

But believing they might be hard evidence I pocketed them.

So what did they have to do with Danny Small? Or me? Melanie. Of course. I glanced again at the photographs, sickened by all that they portrayed. The subjects were all very young, all female, all foreign.

He could never have risked such dangerous tastes in this country. Except once.

And if either the police or the British Medical Association even had a suspicion that Neil had the predilection for such rare delicacies he would be lucky to escape prison and certainly he would *never* practise medicine again.

And although I was no nearer knowing *where* Petra had gone I knew *why*. And Sandy had inevitably followed.

So now I wondered. Had it all started with a child in a pretty dress, meandering through the wood, on a hot, summer's morning, early, before anyone else was about? Had that set an evil taste? Or had it all been there before?

And what had Danny to do with it? Why had Neil killed him? To divert me or to annihilate him? I needed proof, something more than these pictures. They were in themselves, nothing but an indicator. An offence but a less serious one. It was only I, with a ten-year-old daughter that he had skilfully inched towards, who perceived the true malevolence behind them. I could read the fear in the children's eyes and see in them the reflection of the depths of depravity. And I knew that if he could hide all this so cleverly, for so many years, I should fear him. You see Robin had been one person, imperfect but readable. There had been nothing cleverly hidden about my soon-to-be-ex-husband. But Neil was two people, a man to teach your daughter how to play chess, and a monster, whose face I would not recognise. And I wanted to see him convicted for both crimes. Incredibly I was rising up in Danny's defence. *Defend those who cannot defend themselves.*

But I had no proof. This whole solution existed only in my imagination. I must get that proof whatever it cost me. And I would have to work to get it.

Through inanimate objects sometimes answers come. Sometimes not. Like the child's rucksack. Is all this also superstition, this talk of divination? Or is there truth in this particular superstition? That night I again spilled its contents out onto the dining table. In ignorance and innocence Rosie watched me. 'Whose things are they, Mum?'

'A little girl's.'

'Doesn't she want them any more?'

'No.' Mercifully she did not ask anything else but she too glanced through the pile of clothes, underwear, spare shoes, socks. Even her sponge bag was there, toothbrush, Punch and Judy toothpaste, flannel with Barbie embroidered in the corner. All had been packed by loving hands. Vera's, I guessed. Right at the bottom of the sponge bag was a tiny bottle of nasal spray. I picked it up and unscrewed the cap, recognising its contents. So little Melanie Toadstool had suffered from hayfever. I pictured her, eyes streaming in the country air, blistering pollens compared with London. The child must have reacted to the pollens blowing into the house and her grandmother had consulted a doctor.

I sat up. *Consulted a doctor.* That had been how Neil had met her. As simple as that. The child had been brought to him suffering from hayfever and he had prescribed a nasal spray. It wasn't much but it was a new line of enquiry for the police to pursue. I put it back in the rucksack and prepared to give it to Detective Inspector Angela Skilton when next she interviewed me.

Chapter Twenty-one

December 23rd

It was a bad day. Because I had discounted Pritchard I had forgotten about him. It was a mistake. He gatecrashed my evening surgery. I was late finishing anyway, being on call. The run up to Christmas is a doctor's nightmare. Everyone wants to be well for Christmas. So the slightest snuffle or feeling of vague illness is squashed in between the trips to the shops and the supermarket.

See how they still dance around me?

Pritchard began by telling me the police had called round. Two days before his first lone Christmas they had told him the results of the toxicology report, that his mother had died from ingesting a poisonous fungus, *Amanita virosa,* the Destroying Angel.

And he was angry. With me. 'They said you had suggested it might have been that.' He looked puzzled. 'How could you know?'

I didn't mention the long ago doctor's scribble. 'It was a guess.'

He frowned. 'Well, why couldn't you leave her alone? Asking all those questions. She knew what you thought. For years she had forgotten about him. Then you come along. Asking asking asking things you didn't need to know. It was none of your business. He was a cruel man. We were well rid of him. He suffered no more than he deserved. I remember him and the fear he brought into our home and I was only six years old when he died. He gave us hell, my mother and I. An eye for an eye. A tooth for a tooth. It was justice. My mother and I were quite happy together till you tried to spoil it. I liked you, Harriet.' He didn't even pause for breath. 'I came specially to see you because I liked you. I

212

saw you dropping your little girl off outside the school right at the beginning of the year I saw how sad you looked and I thought we could be friends. I thought you *were* my friend. You always seemed so pleasant to me. I knew your husband had left you for another woman and I felt sorry for you. We both had difficulties but I still liked you. I even thought,' he sucked in a noisy breath, 'I thought I could have helped you.'

Had I not been so distraught at my current circumstances I might have laughed at the thought of Pritchard helping me 'get over' Robin. But I didn't feel like laughing during any part of that final day.

'The police told me,' he continued, 'that when the family doctor feels unable to issue a death certificate the usual course of events is to have a post mortem.'

I felt bound to defend myself. 'Look, Mr Pritchard. I'm sorry. I'm so sorry. But as I've pointed out to you before, I was unable to issue a death certificate. Neither was the hospital. And your mother having died within twenty-four hours of admission they had no option but to authorise a post mortem, whatever my opinion. After that the coroner's office had to take that course.'

At least part of my politeness was an apology because in one area I had misjudged him. I had been partly wrong about him.

He hadn't finished with me. 'I'll be straight with you, Harriet. I blame you for my mother's untimely death.'

'Mr Pritchard!'

He was unperturbed. 'I do because it was you who destroyed her.'

'How?'

'You made us remember.'

'You mean your father's death?'

He nodded, used a fat forefinger to wriggle his glasses up his nose. They must be heavy with such thick lenses.

'My mother . . .' To my amazement Pritchard's eyes were

filling. 'She was–' he swallowed. 'She made a dish for my father and he ate it.'

'And it contained?'

'She gave him the Destroying Angel. It was a fungus, poison. For years we had forgotten about it, put it right to the back of our minds. Without his bullying influence our lives have been happy. And then you come along asking questions about how he'd died. No one else was interested. Even at the time of his death people might have guessed it wasn't an accident. But they didn't say anything. No one asked.'

'And your mother's death?'

'The same,' he said.

'But your mother was infirm. She was incapable of harvesting the fungus herself.' I could have added that I knew where it grew at the base of a beech tree miles from Gordon's Lane.

Pritchard nodded. 'She asked me to collect them for her. She didn't tell me why.'

'So you gave them to her?'

'Oh yes,' he said. 'I gave them to her.'

'And she ate them.'

Pritchard took his glasses off so I could see the plump eyelids sagging with grief and tiredness. 'You can call it what you like, Doctor, but I know it was suicide. I never fed them to her. She must have eaten them when I was out at work. All I know is I came home. The dish was empty and she was ill. Very ill. Dying. I feel . . .' He licked his lips. 'I believe that she took them as a sort of atonement for what she had done. Maybe now the Lord will forgive her.'

'Why didn't you tell me this when I visited her?'

Pritchard took a long time to answer when he did there was certain air of fatalism about him. 'I thought if I told you what she'd taken you might know what to give her to prevent her dying. And that wasn't what she'd wanted. She'd made her decision.'

214

'But you collected a poisonous fungus for her *knowing* she was intending suicide? You colluded with her?'

'I didn't know then what she was intending. She just asked me if they still grew at the base of the beech tree towards the middle path through the wood. I told her yes and she said they'd always fascinated her and she wanted me to pick some. She never *actually* said.'

And now we were both silent. But I did not need to shoulder the guilt for Amelia Pritchard's death, suicide or murder.

He did.

'You have to tell the coroner how it happened. Maybe he'll record a verdict of misadventure, Mr Pritchard.'

'Maybe,' he said. 'Maybe not.'

He put his pasty face near to mine before crossing his legs carefully. 'There is another matter.'

My heart sank.

'The headmaster told me you'd been to the school, making suggestions about me. They're untrue. In fact nothing could be further from the truth. I tell you, Harriet. I love children. I love them. I love to be near them. What harm is there in that?'

I couldn't answer him – now.

'Don't go there again,' he said, 'making trouble. It's my job and people might start believing things.'

'Don't worry,' I said.

I waited then for him to go but Pritchard was a strange fellow, capable of doing the most unexpected things. He fished around on the floor and drew out a badly-wrapped parcel in crumpled paper.

'I wanted to show you there's no hard feelings,' he said. 'It's Christmas and therefore a time for forgiveness. You are on your own with your little girl, no doubt missing your husband and I will be missing my poor mother.'

For one awful moment I thought he was going to invite

himself for Christmas dinner and held my breath to make the refusal.

Instead he pushed the parcel across the desk. 'I've brought you a present,' he said. 'To cheer you up, Harriet.' His eyes were on me. 'Go on,' he said. 'Open it.'

I didn't need to. Through the paper I could smell the stale, charity shop smell. I muttered something about waiting till Christmas but he sat and watched me and I knew he wouldn't leave until I had opened it. Reluctantly I tore the paper. It was the navy and white crimplene dress, carelessly folded, the one that had reminded me so forcefully of my mother.

I thanked him and tried to hide unsuccessfully the sudden flood of depression.

I was on call that night, answering queries from worried parents, visiting one or two minor emergencies. I sent an old lady into hospital with heart failure. At midnight I went to bed with my pager propped up against the bedside lamp.

But even before I had gone to sleep it bleeped. I switched the lamp on and read the message.

Melanie Carnforth, aged six. Needs a doctor.

And underneath was the address.

Gordon's Lane.

I gripped the pager, reread the message. I must be having a nightmare. A terrible, terrible nightmare. The child was becoming an obsession.

I read through the message again. It was the same.

Melanie Carnforth, aged six. Needs a doctor.
Gordon's Lane.

I threw the covers off and pulled my clothes on. The child was summoning me. *Not the child. Not the child. The child is dead.*

And like the beat of a drum the words came. If not the child, then who?

I slipped the pager into my coat pocket. This was a taunt from a murderer who thought he was safe. I could go, take the risk, learn things, or I could stay here, also safe, out of harm's way. Would I be out of harm's way? Would I be safe if I stayed here, knowing things? If I didn't go I might *never* know what had happened to Melanie. Therefore I had no choice. I *must* go.

I *would* go. But not unarmed. From the knife block I selected the largest, sharpest knife. I would use it to threaten him and to defend myself. I fondly believed I would bring him in, like a bounty hunter, to confess his crime, both the murder of the child and the killing of Danny Small. And then I could claim my reward, freedom from the charge of unlawful killing.

Upstairs Rosie was asleep. Sylvie was too. I envied them.

I locked the front door behind me. And then I drove along the familiar route, to the south of the town, turning left into the forest. I crossed the causeway over the Heron Pool and watched my headlights glide across the water. Then I climbed. And all the time I was consumed with the fiercest hatred.

Perhaps that was why I missed things.

I pulled the car up in the yard. Pritchard's house was silent and black. I switched my car headlights off and waited for my eyes to adjust. The dull mist had obliterated both stars and moon but I could see a dark shape leaning against the gate. He was waiting for me.

I grasped the knife and memorised my anatomy class again. To kill, to maim, to protect. I would do whatever needed to be done. A flash of the waiting body, skin, blood, bone. An upwards thrust would find the heart even through the protection of the rib cage.

217

I felt cold, detached and awake. The year had finally led to this. I swear I would have done it. I moved towards him.

I know now that he too had a knife. But I never saw it.

Yet I smelt it. You see cold steel has a distinctive scent to it, something metallic and pungent. Or am I still talking about the scent of fear?

When he spoke his voice was ordinary.

'I knew you'd come,' he said with grudging respect.

'You bastard,' I said.

He sighed, world-weary. 'I want the photographs back, Harriet.'

'Those poor children,' I said. 'Tarted up like whores? In their knickers? Wearing lipstick? Frightened? You bastard, Neil. You utter bastard.' Something snapped inside me. 'And what plans did you have for Rosie?'

He said nothing.

I shrieked at him then. 'What were you going to do with my daughter? The same as you did to Melanie? She trusted you, Neil. You were the doctor. You made her better. You abused that position of trust. You bloody well killed her.' I felt sick with hatred, driven to continue. 'You raped her, before you killed her, didn't you? So was that the start of your new taste? And those vulnerable children driven by poverty, hunger. In all the countries of the world? Cheap – aren't they? The price of a slice of bread?'

He said nothing.

'Where have you buried her?'

Again he said nothing. I can only think in his defence that he did not even try to feed me one. He knew his actions were indefensible.

I touched the damp rail of the gate. 'But why Danny, Neil?'

'He saw me,' he said wearily, 'stuffing the dress into the hedge. He said nothing at the time. He was only a kid. He

218

probably didn't understand the significance of what he'd seen. And no one questioned him. But years later he came to the surgery for something and recognised me. To be honest, Harriet, I didn't know what to do. Anyway, I had no record in this country. I don't think the police would necessarily have believed him. And it didn't cost me anything. A few prescriptions,' he said contemptuously. 'That's all.'

'And Petra?'

Neil gave a dry cough. 'Let's just say Petra had her suspicions.'

'Not about Melanie?'

'No, not about Melanie. She would have told the police if she'd known anything about Melanie. She just knew something was wrong.' Again that dry cough. 'The funny thing was that Sandy picked up on something too. He knew something was wrong though I'm pretty sure Petra didn't actually say anything to him.'

I couldn't believe his voice was so normal. We could have been discussing a patient. I tried again. 'Where can I find her body?'

I heard soft footsteps, then Pritchard struck.

I had not heard him. The first I knew was a waft of body odour, the rush of air as his arm was raised and the crunch as he struck Neil's head.

In films they use a cabbage to mimic the sound. They are right. Struck hard enough the human skull will turn as soft as a raw cabbage.

Neil sank with a groan. Pritchard and I were left to face each other across a black void.

'He would have killed you,' he said, 'Harriet.' And for the first time I did not care that he called me *Harriet*. He gripped my hand. 'Now do you trust me?'

I was too shocked to speak.

'Trust me, please.'

'What are you doing here?'

'I heard his car approach. Then yours. I wondered what you were doing out so late. I thought it must be a secret meeting.'

I opened my mouth to speak. Not one word came out.

'Then I heard you quarrelling. I thought he might hurt you. I wanted to protect you.'

'Why?'

He shuffled his feet. I could picture his face. Lardy, pale, sweating with embarrassment.

'I'm a lonely man, Harriet. I don't make friends easily. But you became my friend.'

'I'm your doctor,' I said.

'You talked to me like a friend. You *felt* like my friend. Now you know I had nothing to do with that little girl surely you can *be* my friend.'

My mouth was too dry to say anything.

And I knew Pritchard was smiling.

'You did things for me. Personal things. And for the first time I've done something for you. I've helped you, Harriet. You should thank me really. I've protected you. He would have hurt you.'

The words. *Any* words stuck in my throat.

I glanced down at the dark, immobile shape on the floor.

I believed Neil dead after such a blow. I wanted him dead.

He deserved to die.

I had no pity left in my heart. My pity was for the children of the photographs. For Melanie and those other children in other countries whose abuse was never registered. Perhaps I should have left him lying there.

But I was a doctor. Such behaviour was against my Hippocratic oath. Therefore I was forced to do something. So I did what I must. I knelt beside him. I found his radial pulse, feeble but present. I rolled him into the 'recovery position' and went inside Pritchard's shack to ring for an ambulance while he watched in stunned, uncomprehending immobility.

But Neil was my patient now.

And in the wake of the ambulance came the police to finally take Pritchard away from me, into custody. And an hour later I was forced to face Angela Skilton's sharp questioning. Sceptical and disbelieving. My evidence was weak. Photographs I *claimed* to have found hidden in my partner's consulting room? A hayfever spray I *said* had come from the dead child's rucksack?

But when I told her to check with the paging service and recall my summons to Gordon's Lane I finally watched her attitude change.

Even she could not believe a dead child had called me out there tonight.

'But why,' she asked. 'If he knew you had discovered his dirty little secrets why lure you out here?'

I smiled. Not so clever after all. 'Pritchard would have made a perfect scapegoat,' I said. 'And who would have believed him?'

'Not I,' she admitted. 'When we walked in and saw him sitting in the chair.' She swallowed. 'Blood on his hands, his clothes.' She sat quite still for a moment. 'Do you know what he said, Doctor Lamont?'

I shook my head but I could guess.

'He said he had been protecting you.' Again she paused. 'He couldn't believe it when we took him in. I think he thought we would be pleased with him.' She gave a tight, confused smile before reverting back to the subject of Neil. 'Your partner was a clever man, Doctor Lamont. I would like to see him stand trial.'

But I would not.

I would prefer him to die.

He deserves to die as Pritchard deserves his undoubted plea – of diminished responsibility – and his undoubted fate: following psychiatric assessment to be committed to an institution for an indeterminate length of time. Perhaps until he dies.

But they say Neil will live. Live and face trial? Or merely exist in a vegetative state?

Another fungus feeding on rotting matter?

No one knows yet what will be his prognosis. The medical profession is notoriously cautious and slow. But I am told that Detective Inspector Angela Skilton watches his bed with a puzzled concentration. She still asks herself why these events all happened.

And if we must distrust a doctor then who can we rely on?

Who indeed?

Chapter Twenty-Two

It was more than six months later; on a warm July day that the final chapter of the story was written. At a point not far from the fairy ring of fly agarics in the centre of the wood, an oak tree, rotten for years, toppled after a dry spell and with the wide spread of soil grasped in its roots exposed a small, shallow hole, long enough only for a child's body, now decayed into an anatomy class, bones, some skin, fragments of hair and nails. A hair ribbon.

The child that was lost is found.